a sweet sports romance

BEST FRIENDS BACKUPS & SOMETHING MORE

Raneé S. Clark

Copyright © 2023 by Sweetly Us Press, LLC

All rights reserved

No part of this book may be reproduced in any form whatsoever without prior written permission of the publisher, except in the case of brief passages embodied in critical reviews and articles. This is a work of fiction. The characters, names, incidents, places, and dialogue are products of the authors' imaginations and are not to be construed as real.

Cover design by Sweetly Us Press

Editor: Jenna Roundy

Published by Sweetly Us Press

www.sweetlyuspress.com

CHAPTER 1
ELI

I can't help watching Courtney Edwards from across the gymnasium at Reagan Academy. Not in a creepy way. We spent twenty minutes together earlier today, packing hygiene kits for a nearby women's shelter, before she got enticed away to help another group. Reagan is a private school, and while the kids were here, the room was rowdy and fun. How could it not be with two dozen L.A. Rays players and a hundred teens? The teachers, though ... they're not as fun. Except Courtney. The other teachers seemed, I don't know, too good to be impressed by pro football players? And I don't need people to fawn over me or anything, but Courtney was cool about it. When I'd introduced myself, she'd said, "Oh, right. The quarterback the Rays just signed." She smiled, so welcoming and genuine that I liked her right away.

I want to talk to her now, but I'm second-guessing myself. She clearly knows the other teachers and adults who are standing around the gym in groups, chatting with the players who are still here. But she's sitting by herself, her legs dangling off the low stage at the head of the gym, her gaze jumping between her phone and the people around her. Is she sitting by herself because she wants to be alone?

These thoughts are new and weird for me. As one of the most highly recruited high school quarterbacks and then fourth-round draft pick five years ago, I've had confidence to spare most of my life. But ever since the Arizona Cobras cut me, that's taken a big hit. I've been second-guessing a lot of things lately. Like if I even have a shot here in L.A.

I pick up a couple cans of grapefruit sparkling water that she mentioned liking in the short exchange we had about both of us moving to L.A. recently, and stride toward her. Fake it 'til you make it.

Courtney looks up when I get a few steps away. "Hey, Eli. How's it going?"

I ignore the stupid way my heart pounds. "Good. Thirsty?" I hold out one of the cans of sparkling water to her and sit down.

"Thanks!" She beams at me, her eyes saying she's impressed I remembered. I give myself a little mental pat on the back. Starting off good.

Of course, my football career started off that way too …

I shake that off. No need to let my failures right now infect everything in my life.

She pops the top of the sparkling water and takes her first sip, scrunching her nose. I hide my smile behind my first drink. It's tart, and the carbonation gives it a little bit of a bite. I keep my expression smooth, but she grins at me anyway.

"The first drink always seems to take me by surprise. I don't know why." She laughs and takes another drink. "This was cool. Do you guys do stuff like this a lot?" She gestures around the gym where we were all working half an hour before.

"Most teams do something like this about once a month, sometimes more. This is my first one with the Rays, but the Cobras did it once or twice a month while I was with them." The days we spend in the community, giving back, are some of my favorites. I probably judged the adults here too harshly for their "too cool for this" attitudes, my insecurities pricking. I bet they had fun too.

"What was your favorite volunteer experience?" She sets her can aside and leans back on her hands.

I know that answer immediately. "When we do camps for kids who wouldn't get those opportunities otherwise." I was lucky to have parents who could afford to put me on teams when I was young and pay for me to go to camps. If a kid loves the sport, I want them to have something like that, even if it's just a little bit, to get them going.

She nods. "Teaching something you love to kids is pretty special." She looks around the room again, a smile on her face, but her eyes don't quite match it.

"First year at this school?" I guess. We already chatted about both being new to L.A.

"Yeah. I've been in trainings with everyone, of course." I recognize the nerves in her that have been plaguing me for months.

"Starting somewhere new is never easy."

"I bet you know." We share a commiserating look.

"Well, look at us." I elbow her softly and motion between us. "We both already have at least one new friend."

She raises her eyebrows. "The new quarterback for the Rays wants to be buddies with me?"

I have to laugh. It's hard to imagine beating out Tucker Jones for the starting spot. He's had a rough year, but nothing like my first starting year with the Cobras. I mean, obviously. One year at the helm and then they booted me.

"What?" she questions, tilting her head.

"We're in L.A. Half this room is probably more famous than me. Wasn't that guy in a show with Ben Affleck?" I point to a random teacher, and she shakes her head at me. "You're probably a drama teacher, right?" I go on. "Already a few good roles under your belt, waiting for your big break." I scratch my chin and pretend to study her. She has light-brown hair, pulled into a bun on her head, and in such tight curls that a few can't help springing out here and there. Her golden-brown eyes sparkle as she shakes her head at me.

"I'm a history teacher," she says dryly.

"That's what they all say." I scoff.

"You won't even remember my name once the season starts." She nudges me with her elbow, sitting back up to take a few more sips of her sparkling water. I don't actually like the grapefruit flavor. There's no sugar, so there's nothing to tone down the sourness, but I drink more as well.

"Guess we'll have to hang out more to make sure I do." I swallow back the nerves that attack after I'm bold enough to suggest that. I can picture myself being able to confide in her in a way I don't feel like I can with anyone in my life right now, except my mom. And I've held back a lot from her because I don't want her to worry. My sister Mila is giving her enough gray hairs as it is.

"I wouldn't turn down my only friend," she says.

I'm probably just imagining that she put a very slight emphasis on the friend part, or that her gaze darting away toward one of the groups of teachers is anything more than the same anxious thoughts buzzing through my brain. I called her my friend first, and I definitely didn't do it to put her in the friend zone.

I pull out my phone and hand it to her after unlocking it and opening the messaging app. "Can I have your phone number?"

She takes it with a small smile. "Only if I can have yours," she teases, tapping out something on the screen before handing it back as her own phone dings. She's sent a text to herself that says "Eli Dash."

It would be a simple thing to ask her out for dinner. As friends. I can hang back in that zone until I know for sure she likes me too. Her phone dings with another text as I'm about to let the words spill out, for better or worse, and she stands up.

"I've got to go," she says, and she bites her lip for a second before smiling at me. "We'll definitely hang out again?"

I nod. It's the one thing I'm sure about right now. I want to see her again for sure, friends or whatever. "Absolutely."

Court: First day of training camp tomorrow. Are you ready?
Eli: I'm probably going to die.
Court: You're a professional football player. I've seen your muscles. You will be just fine.
Eli: You're using your teacher voice, aren't you?
Eli: It's the heat. I'll die of heat stroke.
Court: You played for Arizona. In Phoenix…
Eli: I know. I've died of heat stroke before. This is my ninth life, which is why I'm concerned.
Court: You're not a cat.
Eli: That's exactly why I'm concerned. Do I have nine lives? Do I have more?
Court: *rolling-eyes emoji* *laughing emoji* I'm beginning to under-

stand why you've been here for over a month now and I'm still your only friend.
Eli: You've met Mila's friends. Despite their intense efforts, there is no future that direction.
Court: I've been told that Gianna can be anyone you want her to be.
Eli: *face-slap emoji*
Court: Actresses. Am I right, man? *fist-bump emoji*
Eli: Save me.

CHAPTER 2
COURT

I chuckle at Eli's latest text and look up to note that the handful of teachers around me are settling back into chairs after the short break during our curriculum meeting. Nose back to the grindstone.

It's hard to concentrate, though, because we've been going at it most of the day now. My mind wanders to Eli's texts. We've been texting back and forth for weeks, ever since we met at the service project the Rays players did with Reagan Academy's juniors and seniors last month. I can't deny it—his friendship has made settling into L.A. a lot easier. We've bonded over a bunch of things, and not just being new in town and the self-doubt that comes with that. The year hasn't even started, and I'm already trying to prove myself at the prestigious job my aunt got me at Reagan. Eli has a lot to come back from after the losses with the Cobras and getting cut from their team before his contract with them was up. Plus, we both live with actresses at the moment—me with my aunt and Eli with his sister. We always have a lot to talk about.

"Let's move on to the first semester assessment. Last year we had a lot of students who got Some Mastery and Low Mastery on standards 10.1 and 10.2. How are you guys covering that?" Oliver's question is to the whole group, but it snaps my attention up to him. I've been avoiding looking at him directly most of the day. He keeps catching me every time I do. Then he gets this tiny smile, and I blush. We're never going to be able to keep our thing a secret if that continues. Aunt Sophie pulled a lot of strings to get me this job, and if I get booted for dating a co-worker, my dad will never let me hear the end of what a disappointment I am. Not only a teacher, but a bad one at that. He won't be satisfied until I'm superintendent someday, or better yet, the Secretary of Education.

I haven't had a lot to contribute to the meeting so far. I taught at a rural high school in a small Wyoming town for the last few years, where my approach feels different to what the upper-class kids that go to Reagan will need. Wyoming social studies standards are different from California's, and I'm still trying to get a hang of those. Being in the trainings and curriculum meetings has helped, but I'm not ready to offer ideas yet.

The half dozen teachers at the table with me are talking about the various ways they're working with kids on comparing Judeo-Christian views with Greco-Roman views, and I jot down notes on my laptop. Mrs. Burke, the oldest teacher in our group at somewhere over fifty, has the best idea. She had her kids give "missionary" presentations, each having to explain the views of the religion they were assigned as though they were a missionary of the time period. I can't help checking out her kids' scores on the assessment Oliver is talking about. It's no surprise that their scores are higher than the average on that standard.

A new message pops up on my laptop at the same time my phone vibrates in my pocket, and since it's from Eli, I open the messaging app on my computer that syncs with the one on my phone.

Eli: Can we hang out tonight? I hate to invite myself over, but Mila and some friends are doing a Jane Austen reading or something to help prepare one of them for a movie audition.

I wish I could, but Oliver and I are driving over to Malibu for dinner. We can't go out anywhere around Brentwood, where I live with my aunt. A lot of the kids we teach have parents who live nearby, and someone would see us for sure. Without other teachers from the school with us, it would definitely look suspicious.

Court: Sorry! I can't tonight.

Court: The guesthouse is still empty. My aunt wouldn't care if you came over to hang out there for some peace and quiet. You know she has a crush on you.

I try to ignore Eli's response and listen to the other teachers, but we're going on six hours now. My brain has mostly turned to mush, and the economics teacher, Mr. Brewer, is trying to tell the history teachers how they're covering the Crusades wrong.

I click back into the messages. Eli has sent a blushing GIF followed by a laughing emoji.

Eli: If you really think she won't care, I might take you up on that. I need a good night's rest before camp starts tomorrow, and I never know how long Mila and her friends will practice.

Eli needs to get his own place, but he's trying to save money. He has it in his head that his football career is on the rocks and he's on his way out, so he doesn't want to dig into his savings for his housing. I don't know enough about his previous contracts to understand how cheap he's being. Nor have I watched a lot of football. Aunt Sophie was married to a pro football player once, and she's been looking up a ton of stuff about Eli since we started hanging out. She says his problems in Arizona were because his offensive line didn't protect him like they should, whatever that means.

Court: She won't care. Just don't tell her you're there. If you do, there will be no peace and quiet to speak of.

Eli: I don't consider long discussions on passing routes to be a disruption.

I send a rolling-eyes emoji and turn my attention back to the meeting. Someone has distracted Mr. Brewer, and the discussion has turned to which standards we're going to prioritize this year. I have to focus now. My students' scores will suffer if I don't emphasize the same standards as the rest of the department.

Have I mentioned I need to prove I deserve this job at a prestigious private school?

Thankfully, about half an hour later, Reagan's director of education, Violet Avery, tells everyone to start wrapping it up. I mouth "thank you," at her and she grins. One thing to rest at ease about is already having a friend like Violet at the school.

As the teachers at my table pack up their laptops and clean up snack bags and drinks from the area, Violet comes over to me. "Plans tonight?" she asks.

Sheesh. What made tonight the night that everyone wants to

hang out? "Yeah." I grimace at her, hoping she won't ask too many questions.

"Eli, of course," she guesses with a laugh.

I sneak a glance at Oliver, who can obviously hear our conversation, but I can't correct her. I hate lying to Violet about me and Oliver, but since she's an admin at the school, I have to keep her from finding out.

I don't say anything as I put my laptop in my backpack. "Do you have meetings tomorrow?" I ask, once I have the computer stowed. "We could do lunch?"

"No meetings. Let's plan on it." Violet starts walking with me out of the lunchroom, where the teachers were meeting in groups about curriculum.

I glance back at Oliver, who shrugs at me. I'll see him soon enough anyway. I wish we didn't have to keep our relationship a secret. It would be nice to have him hug me and tell me everything's going to be alright when I start teaching here next month.

After one of my first training sessions here, I went out with Oliver and a bunch of other teachers. I really hit it off with him, despite him being almost ten years older than me. He's a history teacher, like me, and we couldn't stop talking about a couple of history accounts we both follow on TikTok and how we wanted to use some fun stuff like that in our classrooms. He teaches seventh- and eighth-grade history, but he's the social studies department head, so it definitely felt good to have him approve of the ideas that had been a success for me at my old school. We made plans to meet up again, and that's when Oliver broke the news to me that it was against Reagan policy for teachers to date. We tried to keep things just friendly, but when it was clear we were both into each other, we decided to date secretly to see what happens and then address the next step when it comes to that.

"How'd your planning go?" Violet asks. "Helpful, I hope?"

From the corner of my eye, I see Oliver fall into step with Mr. Brewer behind us. Oliver meets my eye and smiles, but I turn away. Walking right next to Violet means I have to be extra careful.

"Yes, very helpful," I reply. "I still feel like a fish out of water, though. There's a lot of pressure at a private school like this."

Violet waves this away. She's only a few years older than me, but she landed the admin job at Reagan after barely a couple years of teaching. Oliver says her master's thesis on teacher professional development in the digital age blew everyone away, and she was a shoo-in when the old director of education left to take a job at UCLA.

"You came from a good school, rural or not, Court," she says. "I looked up the scores there after you interviewed, and it's impressive what they're able to do with the resources they have. You're not a fish out of water here. Stop sweating it." She reaches over to squeeze my elbow reassuringly. Maybe it's not the same as having a hug from Oliver, but it does ease some of the tightness in my chest.

"I'll try." We've reached the hallway where Violet needs to split off to go to her office while I head out to the parking lot.

"See you tomorrow?" she says as she heads off toward her office with a wave. She doesn't wait for my response.

I walk out the doors to the staff parking lot, purposefully not looking over my shoulder to see what Oliver and Mr. Brewer are doing.

Footsteps hurry toward me as I step up to my car. "Still on for tonight?" Oliver asks in a low voice, only stopping at the hood of my car and not getting too close. Still, his smile makes my knees a little weak, and I can't help thinking of the gentle way he cradled my cheek in his hand when he kissed me goodbye on the last date we were on.

"Of course." I keep my smile neutral, especially as Mr. Brewer walks by with Mrs. Burke. Thankfully, they only glance at us and smile back before splitting to go to their own cars.

"Can't wait," Oliver says. He holds my gaze, and I'm pretty sure we're both feeling the longing to close the distance between us. My brain goes to the first time he held my hand, the way warmth jumped through me when his fingers slid down into mine and he gently tugged me closer to him.

"Me either," I say, and my voice is soft and sounds silly to my ears, but I can't help it.

Oliver winks at me before he pulls himself away and jogs to his car.

I get into my own car and then gaze at him as he slips into his Kia EV6. It's electric, which he's talked a lot about, especially anytime we drive my Jeep Cherokee. It might be the age difference and an unconscious habit to teach me or something. He doesn't quite understand what *rural Wyoming* means, but I'll take him to visit the little town I taught in someday and he'll see why I needed four-wheel drive.

I chide myself for getting too far ahead. The thing between me and Oliver isn't serious.

I smirk. Yet.

CHAPTER 3
ELI

I've had the gate code for Sophie Edwards's house for over two weeks now. Court insisted so I don't have to use the call button every time I come and alert her aunt to my presence. It makes me laugh that Court is protective of my time, like her aunt is some rabid fan she has to run interference for. The truth is, Ms. Edwards—who has begged me to call her Sophie, and I can't quite bring myself to—is fun. She knows a lot about football, which isn't surprising, considering she was married to Russ Ano for ten years before he died. The guy was a legendary receiver for the Vegas Vipers. Sophie was also my mom's favorite romcom actress back in the day. It's a little surreal that Court acts like *I'm* the famous one around here.

Court pulls her car out of the garage as I pull up in front of the guesthouse. She stops and rolls down her window, waiting for me to approach.

"Another teacher thing?" I ask.

She shakes her head. "I've got a date." That would explain the blush creeping up her cheeks.

I make sure not to react. Court is pretty much everything I want in a girlfriend—fun, kind, and easy to talk to. Things are so relaxed between us, and like I predicted, I've shared a lot of my insecurities with her. She's shared hers with me too. I want to explore our connection romantically, but I have to give Court time to figure it out. I don't want to force this with her.

"Then why isn't he picking you up?" I tease.

Court's blush deepens. "It's the twenty-first century, Eli. Come join us."

"Call me old-fashioned." I shrug and smile at her. "I've picked you up every time we've gone out, and we're not even dating." I hope she picks up everything I'm insinuating in that statement. "Who's the lucky guy?" I ask.

"No one you know," she says quickly, and she waves at me. "See you later, Eli!" She pulls away before I can reply. I mean, of course I don't know her date. The guy would have to play for the Rays or be one of Mila's friends for me to know them. I frown after her, wondering what reason she'd have to be cagey with me about the guy she's going out with.

Court always drives with her phone notifications turned off, so I send off a text, knowing that she won't see it until she gets to wherever she's meeting the guy.

Eli: Don't be embarrassed if you met this guy on the internet. It's the twenty-first century, Court. Come join us.
Eli: In all honesty, I just want to make sure you're safe.

I head into the guesthouse, which I also have the code for, thanks to Court. I've spent a few nights here since moving in with Mila. It's a small studio, and I wish I could find something like it without it costing an arm and a leg. Housing in Arizona was so much cheaper, and with my future in flux, I don't want to blow what I have now because I want a better place. Given my past with the Cobras and my shaky future, my $900,000-a-year contract is better than I could have hoped for. If I end up being the starting quarterback—something I can't quite bring myself to believe will happen—there will be bonuses and eventually a new contract. But only $200,000 of this contract is guaranteed. I need to at least secure the backup quarterback position to feel more stable. And after everything that happened last year and a 3–14 season that most people give me a good chunk of the blame for, that feels out of reach. Mila has chided me that my insecurities from last year are tainting everything, making me a miser with my money when I didn't used to be. Not that I ever spent lavishly. Between me and Mila, I've always been the responsible one with money, saving my allowances and then the meager amounts of money from the few summer jobs I could get because football was the number one priority. I'm not sure I can trust money management advice from a woman who's gone through four different careers in the last five years.

Maybe I do need to go inside the main house and talk to Ms. Edwards. She'd make me feel better about football and my position with the Rays. Court gives great pep talks, and I know where she gets her talent from. If I stay friends with Court, I could see Ms. Edwards quickly becoming a second mother to me. I already have several sentences from her in my "Kind Words" note on my phone. It's a list my mom started for me last season to help me focus on good things and not spiral too much from the criticism everyone had for my playing. She always made sure to text me non-football things too, to point out that my career choice doesn't define me. I've kept it up, and reading back through that list still helps me on low days.

I'm settled on the bed, studying my playbook, when Court texts me back.

Court: I didn't meet him on the internet, and I'm completely safe. You'll be the first to know if I'm not, promise.
Eli: Maybe 911 should be first, then me.
Court: Fair point.

I don't respond. I don't want to be the guy texting a woman while she's out with another guy. Well, I kind of do, but I rise above the temptation to sabotage her date.

I have my dinner delivered—tacos from a place down the street. My sister texts while I'm eating, a photo of her and one of the guys I've seen hang around the apartment with her and her other actor friends.

Mila: Eli. I'm completely in love.

She follows this with at least ten heart-eyed emojis.

Eli: I'm very happy for you.

Mila: We all took a break and went to the coffee place down the street for dinner, and I tripped on this dumb step coming into the apartment, and he carried me up to the apartment after I got hurt.

She adds a GIF of a woman fainting. Swooning, as she would call it.

Eli: Did he play Captain America? I think that's where I recognize him from.

Mila's answer is a face-slap emoji, and then she stops texting. Maybe I should be a better brother and show more enthusiasm, but this is the fifth guy that Mila's fallen completely in love with since we moved to L.A. It's all just another thing for her to try out. She had no interest in acting until I told her and Mom that I'd been signed by the Rays, and then it was a "sign" that she should follow her dream. The dream she'd had since lunchtime the day before.

It's midnight before Court texts that she's back from her date, which I already know. Once it was past eleven, I couldn't help watching out the window for her headlights. The guesthouse sits kitty-corner from the garage, so I had the perfect view anyway.

Eli: Maybe next time we should have a code word.
Court: What are you still doing up? I thought you needed a good night's sleep.
Eli: Studying my playbook. Gotta be prepared for tomorrow.
Court: Trust me, you're going to be fabulous. Say it with me, Eli.

I smile.

Eli: I'm going to be fabulous.
Court: Yeah, you are.

I set aside my playbook and get ready for bed. Tomorrow's going to be a long, stressful day, and now that Court is home safely, I'm going to get the rest I need.

CHAPTER 4
COURT

Let me give it to you straight. Standards and planning around them have never been my strong point, which might have been why I felt so lost during the curriculum planning meeting last week. Well, that and the fact that Oliver is incredibly distracting. He's been doing a summer school session the last week, which is why I've actually been able to get stuff done. It's been a chore to adjust my plans from my old teaching job to the new one at Reagan, but at least I'm not starting from scratch again.

"Are you still at it?"

Aunt Sophie's voice makes me look up from where I have all my stuff spread on her kitchen table. It also alerts me to how stiff my back feels. I glance at my phone. It's almost eight p.m., and I've been working since noon on this.

I sigh. "Yeah. But now is as good a time as any to break for the night." I start gathering things.

"Will you be working on that again tomorrow?" Aunt Sophie asks, going to the fridge and opening it. Her kitchen is huge and open, one of the many luxuries I love about her home. In addition to the twelve-seat table I'm working at, there's a large island and seating there too. Aunt Sophie slips onto an upholstered stool with the cold pizza she pulled from the fridge. I think she's making up for all the dieting she did in her twenties and thirties to keep her spot on the big screen.

"Yeah." I sigh again. The prep work feels never-ending. I can't wait to get back in the classroom.

"Then just leave that. No one else is using the table right now." She offers me a slice of pizza, which I accept, but I take it to the air fryer to warm it up, opening the door to the butler's pantry that runs the length of the kitchen behind the wall with the main counter, stove, and fridge. It's one of the coolest things, with a door disguised as another cupboard. When I was younger, Aunt Sophie would play hide and seek with me in her huge house when I came to visit, and she usually found me quickly because I always thought the pantry was the sneakiest place.

I wait to respond to her until my pizza's done warming up. The air fryer's too loud to hear over anyway, especially back here in the pantry. It's very domestic of me, but I think the air fryer might be my new favorite appliance. I didn't have one in the little house I rented in Wyoming. I've discovered since moving in with Aunt Sophie that I probably won't be able to live without one now.

I get a text from my dad while I'm waiting for my pizza to reheat.

Dad: How's the new school? Read up about some of the powerful graduates from there. You should check some of these out. Great networking opportunities!

He adds a link that I don't click. I know Reagan has produced some impressive alumni. Probably a few politicians on there, high-powered lawyers, and some CEOs for sure. There are even a couple notables from the film industry, which was how Aunt Sophie got me the job. I ignore his obvious pushing me toward the bigger and better he keeps insisting I need and respond to his asking about the school.

Court: It's been mostly meetings and stuff so far, but everyone is nice. Can't wait to get back in the classroom and work with kids again.

I add a heart emoji, wondering if Dad will ever see where my passion is and the reason I went into teaching in the first place. Not to impress him, obviously. I would have gone to work at his software development company and worked my way up to taking over someday.

He doesn't reply before my pizza is done, so I figure his sole purpose was to pass on the names of people he thinks I need to suck up to in order to advance my career. Of course.

I come out from the pantry to find Aunt Sophie leaning on her elbow, eating her pizza cold, and looking like she's almost a normal aunt. She's wearing baggy sweats and a Vegas Vipers T-shirt, her fading blond hair braided down her back. She's aged well, and she's the first to tell you about the little things she does to look more like forty-five than she does fifty-five. A little something to smooth out her forehead, the slightest lift around her eyes, and a little plumping to her lips. She's always told me she never went big into looking young, because she wanted to be an example to me that she could still be successful even while letting nature take its course. Mostly.

"Are you sure about that mess?" I ask, taking a seat away from all my papers to eat my pizza.

She nods. "Claire won't be in until later in the week, so no one will disturb it," she says, talking about her housekeeper. She reaches for another slice of the pizza she got out, wiggling her eyebrows at me. I love the way Aunt Sophie takes such delight in something simple like cold pizza in the evening. I wish I could feel more of that, but the pressure of this job weighs on me too much.

My phone dings, and I cringe, wondering if my dad is going to push this networking thing. But when I glance over to see who it's from, I relax instantly. Eli.

Eli: Tragedy has struck.

My heart lifts at a text from him. He's been so exhausted the last week from training camp that we've barely texted in the evenings when he gets home. I'm sure it's just that Oliver's busy as well that has me feeling a little lonely.

"Eli?" Aunt Sophie guesses with a grin. "Why aren't you making out with that young man yet?"

Because that would be cheating on my secret boyfriend. "We're friends," I remind her instead. I could trust Aunt Sophie with my secret about Oliver, but it's easier to keep it from everyone so I don't have to think too hard about who I can tell and who I can't. That's a recipe for disaster. Not for the first time, I wonder what she'd think about me dating someone who's almost forty. Probably nothing. Her first husband, Russ, was older than her, but only by about five years, but I know she has friends in the business with much larger age gaps than ten years.

"Which seems silly," Aunt Sophie says. This is a regular discussion with us. Russ was a football player and the love of her life. No doubt they'd still be married if he hadn't died young, only forty years old. It was an awful twist of fate—a massive heart attack despite still being in incredible shape. He'd only retired a couple years before.

So I think she believes Eli must be my perfect match because he's a football player. The fact that he's a great guy, friendly and sweet, is a bonus for her.

I shake my head at her, knowing I won't win an argument for why we're just friends, especially given that I can't tell her about my biggest reason. I grab my phone to text Eli back.

Court: Scale of "can't decide what to eat for dinner" to "getting cut," how bad is this tragedy?
Eli: Somewhere in the middle. Mila's decided to move in with a bunch of her actor friends for cheaper rent. Like six of them or something.
Eli: I don't think it's going to last long, which puts me in a pickle.

I snort laugh. Who says stuff like that? I glance up to see Aunt Sophie watching me knowingly. "Just because he's funny doesn't mean I should be dating him."

She rolls her eyes. "It's one of the best reasons." She stands and gathers up her plate and the empty pizza box.

Court: I'm sorry, but … pickle?
Eli: I need to find somewhere to rent, but probably short term. Not an easy task, hence me in a pickle.
Court: You're just going to own it, aren't you.
Eli: I'm committed.

Court: The obvious answer to this is to rent the guesthouse.

Aunt Sophie usually has it rented out, but it's been empty for a couple months. She doesn't need the income. Her second husband, a man who was far too practical for Aunt Sophie, at least made sure her movie paychecks were always earning. Financially brilliant but had every single thing about their relationship scheduled.

You know what I'm getting at. Yes, that.

The dots saying that Eli's typing dance for way too long. Then stop. Then dance some more.

Eli: Would she really be okay with it?
Court: This is Aunt Sophie we're talking about. It's probably her dream come true.

Eli sends a smirking emoji.

"Aunt Soph?"

She's still sitting at the island, watching me shamelessly. "Hmm?"

"Can Eli rent your guesthouse?" I quickly explain about Mila deciding to move out. I don't understand someone making around a million dollars a year feeling like he needs a roommate or cheap rent, but Aunt Sophie seems to get it for some reason. "He's not guaranteed that," she'd said when I brought it up with her. "I don't understand it all either." Then she shrugged.

"Of course." She brightens, her expression turning mischievous.

I narrow my eyes at her. "This means nothing."

"Obviously." She saunters out of the kitchen without even telling me how much she's going to charge him rent. He'll want to know that.

Court: She's 1000% on board, as we knew she would be. Call her tomorrow about the $$ details.
Eli: First friends, and now we're practically roomies. This is moving a little fast for me.

I chuckle. I can't think of a person I'd want to be practically roommates with besides Aunt Sophie.

Okay, maybe Oliver, but that's *really* getting ahead of myself. Still, I can picture cozy evenings on the couch at his house in Encino, talking about our day together at Reagan. He'll be in admin someday soon, I'm sure, but I'll be happy teaching the rest of my life.

Court: I promise not to suffocate you with my neediness.
Eli: Phew. Glad we got that resolved. Most awkward relationship talk ever.

I send him the face-slap emoji that he's so fond of. He says it's because Mila uses it all the time and she's rubbed off on him.

Eli: I'll call tomorrow. Going to bed now. Body shutting down.

I shoo away the disappointment that we didn't get to talk about training camp again. He's only said, "Going good," whenever I ask. No worries. Pretty soon he'll be right next door, practically my roommate, and I'll be able to see for myself how things are going.

It occurs to me that having the guy who's quickly becoming my best friend a few short steps away might not bode well for keeping Oliver a secret from him, but I dismiss that quickly as well. Oliver and I never hang out at Aunt Sophie's anyway, so that won't be a problem.

Keeping Aunt Sophie from matchmaking me and Eli together? That's the real issue.

CHAPTER 5
ELI

Despite Court's comment the other night when I questioned her date's chivalry, I am firmly in the twenty-first century. But as modern as I am, it still comes as a little bit of a surprise that one of Mila's new roommates is a guy. Jack, to be precise. The hero who selflessly carried her up the stairs after her tragic sprained ankle moment.

"You barely know him," I say in a low voice while I carry one of her suitcases up the stairs to the new apartment. "Are you sure this is a good idea?"

"I've known him almost as long as Gianna and Layla," she says, her voice a little condescending.

That's a stretch. She met Gianna and Layla at her first acting class, when we'd been in town for just a couple days. Jack came at least a couple weeks later. "It's different."

Listen, I know my retort is lame.

She scoffs. "Don't be such a prude, Eli." She shakes her head at me the same way Mom did when I backed into the garage door my freshman year of high school. The resemblance between their disappointed looks is uncanny. "There's absolutely nothing going on with me and Jack." She takes a couple steps ahead, but I don't miss the "yet" that she adds to that statement.

I press my lips together to keep from lecturing her. It won't do any good. She'll push harder back at me. I can't help that I feel responsible for her while we're living in L.A. together, even if she is twenty-three and an adult in her own right. I'm her big brother. But I have to let her make her own decisions, even if this one is stupid. He could murder her in her sleep, for all we know. Twenty-first century hip or not, my big brother instincts hate that Jack and another guy I don't know are among the five people my little sister will be sharing an apartment with. My sister gives her heart so easily, all of it, and Jack could take advantage of that.

When I come upstairs with another one of Mila's boxes, there's another guy going inside with a couple boxes of his own. It's not Jack—he dropped off his stuff and then took off—so this must be the other male roommate. I can't remember the name Mila told me. I think that was right about the moment when I was blinking at her and trying to process the fact that she was moving out of our apartment on a whim. I thought the month-to-month contract we accepted was going to be a way for the landlord to raise our rent whenever he wanted, but I'm lucky now it wasn't longer term.

"Hey," the guy says, setting down the boxes in the living room. "I'm Landon. Are you one of the guys moving in here?"

I shake my head. "Mila's brother. You're Jack's roommate?"

His turn to shake his head. "Maybe we should both stop guessing." He chuckles and then sticks out a hand. "I'm Landon, next-door neighbor."

I shift the box I'm holding to shake his hand. "Nice to meet you. I'm Eli."

After I take the box into Mila's room, I come out to find him heading down the hallway. We walk together down the stairs.

"How long have you lived here?" I ask.

"A couple years. I teach economics at Los Angeles City College."

He has a slightly nerdy look that I'm pretty sure isn't Mila's type —loose jeans, a black tee with a joke that I don't get about supply and demand, and a worn-out pair of leather sandals. His hair is neat and short. Hopefully I don't need to worry about him.

"You make friends fast," I say as he greets Gianna when we get to the sidewalk and she hands him another box with a smile.

"Layla—" He gestures to her, grabbing another box out of the back of my SUV. "—is my cousin. I'm the one who let her know this apartment was open."

"Cool."

Mila waves me over, and I nod at Landon, going to retrieve more of her boxes to take upstairs. We chat a little more as we get the women moved in, and I like him. He doesn't follow football, but he's impressed when he finds out I'm a pro football quarterback. I quickly tell him that I'll probably end up as Tucker Jones's backup, and he shakes his head.

"You're good enough to have a pro contract. That's something big. Don't sell yourself short." He pats me on the shoulder and grins. "Promise you'll come play once with my buddies? There's a group that gets together to play flag football on Saturdays sometimes, college friends of mine, and I'm always the worst."

I grin at him. His friendship was offered easily, like Court's, and it makes me like him. "Sure. I'd love to."

"They'll probably know who you are, but maybe we can fake them out at first. Tell them you're someone else." His eyes light up at the idea, and it makes me laugh.

"Yeah, that would be fun." If they know who I am, it's because I got so much bad press last year for all the losses, but I push that away. Landon's excited, and I bet I could at least make him look cool in front of his college friends. When I'm back down in my car after I finish at Mila's, I open up my "Kind Words" note and add the things that Landon said.

I head back to our old apartment to grab my stuff. I don't have very much. I left most of it in storage in Phoenix, just in case, which my mom said was pessimistic. I called it practical. It's only a few boxes, and I have it all transferred to Ms. Edwards's guesthouse in half the time it took to move Mila's stuff—and I did it by myself. Still, it's getting dark by the time I drop onto the couch located in one corner of the guesthouse. Moving all day was not in my plans for my first Saturday off after the start of training camp. Since I'm saving so much by renting this guesthouse, I did splurge on hiring someone to clean up the old apartment rather than worrying about it myself. I'm glad that's all taken care of.

I text Court that I'm officially settled, but I know that she's out with some of the teachers from her school. She'd already made the plans when I let her know I'd be moving and helping Mila move today, and she felt bad that she couldn't help. It was last-minute, so I definitely don't blame her.

Eli: You would be so proud. I made a new friend. His name is Landon, although I might have a type. He's a teacher like you, at Los Angeles City College.
Court: I'm not surprised you're drawn to us. We're both in charge of a bunch of people all going in different directions half the time.

Court doesn't even know the half of me being drawn to her. She's got me so far into the friend zone that I don't know if she'd get that my flirting was real, short of me walking up and kissing her. Does she not feel the spark I do when we talk, and even just through our texting? There's something keeping her back, and I need to figure out what. Living this close to her will definitely help me figure that out, right?

Eli: Stop by tonight for my housewarming party if you're not too late. ;)

CHAPTER 6
COURT

I don't see Eli's texts about being settled into the guesthouse until later, while I'm waiting for Oliver to meet me at the ice cream place he says I can't go another day without trying. I look at my watch again. We split up from the other teachers almost an hour ago and planned to come straight here, but I've been waiting over half an hour for Oliver. We both came from the same place, so I'm not sure what's keeping him.

This ice cream place is a little bougie too. I had to wait to be seated, and thinking that Oliver was right behind me, I got us a table. The waiter has been by multiple times, and I keep telling him that my friend will be here any minute. I texted Eli a while ago that I was still out with friends, so I pull out my phone now to see if he's responded.

Eli: No problem. It might be a lame housewarming party. Just you and me. I forgot to invite my new friend Landon.

Eli is a friendly, likable guy. It's kind of crazy to me that he doesn't hang out more with his teammates or something. There's a draw to him that's hard to resist. He gets so invested in any story I'm telling him that I have honest worries I'll one day spill that Oliver and I are dating because Eli's so easy to talk to.

Court: I'm waiting for my friends to catch up at the fanciest ice cream place I've ever seen. They serve it in courses here. No joke.
Eli: An entire dinner of ice cream. This is my kind of place.
Court: I'd offer to bring you something, but ... melting.
Eli: I appreciate the sentiment.

I want Eli's first night in the guesthouse to be good and welcoming, but if Oliver doesn't get here soon, it will be too late to even drop by for a minute. Eli goes to bed early. He takes his bedtime seriously, and in the month that I've known him, I've only gotten texts from him later than 10:30 p.m. a couple of times.

I glance up to see Oliver at the entrance of the shop, chatting with the hostess. I wave at him as the hostess grabs a couple menus, like Oliver didn't realize I was here. He scowls, looking surprised that I'm already seated.

"When did you get here?" he asks when he slides into the booth across from me. He frowns at me, and it feels like I've messed up somehow, but I don't know why. Even though he's only thirty-eight, nine years older than me, he has the lightest dusting of gray through his brown hair and a few fine lines around his eyes that give away his age. Usually, it's a whole sexy professor vibe, but right now I feel like I'm getting detention or something.

I tilt my head. "I came straight from the bowling alley. Did you get stuck in traffic?"

His frown deepens. "No. Jess was down in San Diego at an education conference last week, and we chatted about it. I didn't realize we were coming straight here." His tone has a definite bite to it, which takes me off guard. "If you were going to come straight here, why didn't you tell me?"

"I ..." The truth is, I'm not sure what to say or why it feels like this misunderstanding is my fault. When Oliver invited me to the bowling alley with some of the other teachers from Reagan, we planned this date in texts before we came. Oliver had said "after we're done," but maybe I was wrong to assume *right* after?

Oliver sighs, sounding long-suffering, and opens his menu. "I hate that you were waiting so long. I don't want to be that guy."

I know he wants to take care of me, so I shoo away the feeling that this is my fault. I'm reading into his reaction because his frustration—with himself—is showing.

The waiter stops at the table. "Are we ready to order?" he asks.

I basically have the menu memorized at this point, and I decided twenty minutes ago on a Belgian waffle topped with cheesecake-flavored ice cream and raspberry syrup. "Yes," I say, and Oliver's frown returns. Okay, yeah, he did just get here, so that was probably premature. I'm feeling defensive about our misunderstanding too, though, and I don't want to back down. I rattle off my order, and when the waiter turns to Oliver, he tells him he's going to need more time.

"Do you want me to bring out yours or wait?" the waiter asks me.

I don't look at Oliver. "Go ahead and bring it out, please."

The waiter nods and walks off, glancing at Oliver over his shoulder. I feel a little vindicated in my attitude when the waiter rolls his eyes. He catches me looking and grins. I hide my own smile and turn away.

"Do you need to be somewhere?" Oliver asks, still scanning the menu. "If I had known—"

"It's fine." I don't want to continue this conversation. Maybe we're both just tired after the three games we bowled with the others. "My friend just moved into Aunt Sophie's guesthouse, and I want to check on him tonight. I didn't realize we were going to be out so late."

Oliver bristles. "Can't your aunt do that?"

She probably already has. I might need to go home and rescue Eli. "He's my friend," I repeat.

Oliver narrows his eyes, and I hope my ice cream comes fast. I'm not sure what's up with him tonight, and I don't like it.

The waiter comes back with my ice cream, and I know he rushed it, especially when Oliver's eyes narrow again at him. "Are you ready?" he asks Oliver.

"Of course." Oliver's voice is definitely chillier. He orders a vegan chocolate avocado ice cream over a gluten- and dairy-free brownie. It strikes me at this moment that I know nothing of Oliver's dietary restrictions. I've never even thought to ask, even though we've been out to restaurants a couple times. Did I miss something before? Maybe I'm the reason we had this misunderstanding—not paying attention.

"He's flirting with you," Oliver says when the waiter walks away. "He brought your order right out. That's never happened to me when I come here."

I shake my head. "He feels bad. He's been checking on me since I got here." I dig my spoon into the very creamy ice cream, making sure to get a generous portion of the perfectly golden-brown Belgian waffle.

Oliver scoffs, and we fall into silence. The ice cream *is* not to be missed. It tastes like the homemade ice cream my grandma used to make for family dinners, perfectly sweet with strong hints of vanilla, and the cheesecake flavoring is on point. The waffle is crispy on the outside, but chewy and delicious inside. Points to Oliver, because I will definitely be coming back. And even though something like chocolate avocado isn't usually my jam, I am a little bit curious about it.

I ask about the conference Oliver spoke with his friend Jess about, and he talks about a couple of the classes while I finish my ice cream. We had burgers and fries at the bowling place, so I'm bursting at the seams, but that dessert was absolutely worth it.

It takes another ten minutes after I finish my ice cream before the waiter brings Oliver's out. I don't doubt that was on purpose. I ask for my check before the waiter leaves, and then look apologetically to Oliver. "Sorry. I need to go." I pull my purse across my lap to grab my credit card, so I'm ready as soon as the waiter gets back. Despite how good the ice cream was, the vibe between Oliver and me has been off since he got here, and I'm eager to leave and start fresh next time we're together.

Oliver watches me, the skin around his eyes tightening even as he takes his first bite of his ice cream. "Is there something going on between you two? You and your friend." He emphasizes the last word the slightest bit so that it's easy to catch his meaning.

The idea that Eli and I are more than friends takes me by surprise. We have so much fun together, but there's nothing romantic. He is very attractive. That all-American, stereotypical jock look is a thing for a reason. He wears his dark hair in a conservative, shorter style, shaved on the sides and a little longer on the top. He told me it's easier when you're wearing a helmet as much as he does. He's tall and muscled, of course. Obviously attractive, but it's so much more than that. He's thoughtful, the kind of guy who waits up to make sure you make it home from a date even if he won't admit that's what he's doing. The guy who worries over his adult sister and the flaky guy she believes she's head over heels in love with, but he's also the guy who still tries to respect her decisions, as much as he disagrees with them.

"No," I say firmly. Thankfully, the waiter is already returning with my check. I hand him my credit card, and he disappears. Oliver and I sit in silence, my irritation growing that he assumes that because I want to be a good friend to Eli, there must be something going on.

"How's your ice cream?" I ask. I have at least a couple minutes before the waiter gets back, and I don't want us to end our date on a completely sour note.

"Delicious, of course. Want to try it?" His tone warms only slightly.

"Not tonight. I'm so full, I don't think I'd appreciate it." I pat my stomach as though that proves my point.

The waiter returns with my card, and I stand as soon as I'm done writing out the tip amount and signing the receipt. I kiss Oliver on the cheek before I leave. "See you later," I say, and then I walk away. Hopefully we'll be able to shake off this funk before we see each other next.

It's 10:15 when I pull into the garage at Aunt Sophie's. I text Eli before I get out of my car. There was a light on in the guesthouse, but maybe he's already in bed and winding down.

Court: Too late to stop by the housewarming party?

His response is immediate.

Eli: Never too late for you.

CHAPTER 7
ELI

Tension hovers around Court when I answer the door at her knock, so I open my arms, hoping she'll accept a hug. She steps into my arms, and as I wrap them around her, I can feel her relaxing into me.

"Everything go okay?" I ask when she steps away, and I close the door.

"Me and another teacher kind of had an off night. It's fine." She waves her hand and moves to the couch, falling down on it. "We're friends. We disagreed about something small, and I felt weird about it." She makes a show of looking around. "I love what you've done with the place."

I chuckle. The guesthouse is furnished, and the only difference I've made is the dark gray blanket and navy pillows that now decorate the bed. I sit down on the couch next to her, letting our legs touch. I want her to feel the heat between us that I know is there along with the comfort we have in each other's company.

Court leans her head on my shoulder, relaxing even more. Maybe that's the problem—the electricity between us is buried by the fact that she's so at ease with me. We've been at ease with each other almost since moment one.

"Can I ask you a hypothetical question?" she asks.

"Of course."

"If you had a girlfriend—"

"Why is that only hypothetical? You think I'm not the boyfriend type?" I tease. Maybe this will help me point out the possibilities that exist between us.

She raises her eyebrows. "Do you have a girlfriend?" she asks.

Would she be jealous if I did? "No. Just you." I wink, and she shakes her head and laughs.

"So *hypothetically*, if you had a girlfriend, what would you think if she had a good friend that was a guy?" She chews on her lower lip, her eyes questioning.

Where is this going? Court doesn't have a boyfriend. I know she would have told me if she did. "I need more information. Like, has she given me a reason to suspect something is going on between them, or it's just that she has the friend?"

She looks down, away from me. "Maybe she mentions wanting to check on him."

"That's it?" The answer feels obvious. "If I was bothered by her friendships with others, the problems would be deeper than jealousy. That's a trust issue—I hope that my hypothetical girlfriend would know that I trust her."

She nods, but she still looks bothered.

"Is this what you and the other teacher disagreed on?" I ask.

She shrugs. "Kind of. I don't want to explain. It's not my place." Her cheeks turn pink, the way they did when she told me about her date last week. "Tell me about training camp. You've hardly said a word."

"Exhausting. We'll start wearing full pads tomorrow, and then it will get more grueling." I grimace at her.

"And how do you feel about your position? Do the guys like you? Do you like the team?" She shifts so that she's sitting sideways on the couch, leaning toward me, her legs crossed in front of her.

"The team is great. Everyone has been really welcoming." More so than I thought. Things are in flux with the Rays. They've made some trades recently to build a better foundation, and everyone knows the quarterback position is the next thing they're nailing down to start the road to building a championship team. As loyal as the team is to each other, there's such a good relationship with the coaching staff and a trust that they'll make the right decisions. The guys accept the choices that are being made. I believe they'd support me if I was named starter. Don't get me wrong, Tucker Jones is a great quarterback, but I used to be too.

"What about the offensive line?" Court asks. "Do they like you? Do you like them?" When I tilt my head at her, confused at this line of questioning, she goes on. "Aunt Sophie says your offensive line was a big problem with the Cobras. They didn't get you the kind of time you needed to make plays."

There was a breakdown in my relationship with the O-line after the first few losses, but I can't lay the blame there. Not entirely. But Ms. Edwards probably did hear the handful of commentators mentioning that the average time I had to pass was lower than any other team in the league.

"Things feel good," I say. "Everyone there seems committed to lifting each other up. Coach keeps saying that a rising tide lifts all boats."

"He's smart," she says. She turns and shifts so that she's leaning against me again. I want to pull her into my arms. "I should go and let you sleep," she murmurs, resting her head against my shoulder.

"It's fine." I don't want her to leave. She's warm against my side and making electricity jump through me. "Tell me about that place where you worked in Wyoming. You always talk about it with so much happiness."

"I loved it there. It was such a tiny town where everyone knew each other. Some people hate that kind of thing, but it was sort of fun to go into the little grocery store and stop to chat with at least three people in what's supposed to be a short trip for milk and bread."

"Sounds a little idyllic." Especially since it feels like the only people I really know here are Court, Mila, and Ms. Edwards. There's the team, but I don't want to get too attached yet. Who knows what could happen this season?

"There are hard things too. There were opportunities that the kids don't have because it's a rural area—not as many clubs and extracurriculars as the bigger schools, so some kids seem to fall through the cracks or don't feel like they belong. I hated stuff like that."

"I get that." I can't help but rest my chin on top of her head for a moment. It feels so right, us together. So at ease on this couch, as though we've been dating for months or years. "I wouldn't be playing pro football today if I hadn't been on an elite team in high school or had the competitive teams I played on year-round when I was younger."

She tilts her head up toward me. I want to lean over and kiss her. "What do you want for your kids? Big cities and opportunity, or idyllic small town?" she asks.

"As long as I'm playing football, the choice is already made." I shrug. "But if I had a choice … Think there's something in between?" I ask softly. She's killing me here. I should ask her on a date, make sure she knows exactly how I feel about her. But I don't know if I can swing and miss with her. That's a rejection I can't take after all the rejection I've faced the last year.

She nods. "The school I taught at competed against some bigger schools nearby on occasion. Places that still had that smaller-town feel but had bigger schools and were closer to larger cities. I think that's maybe what I want too, but …" She trails off. She's mentioned before that she has to succeed at Reagan and that she feels a lot of pressure from her family to do something big.

"Court?" I lean back to look at her. "I would never presume to tell you how to deal with your family, but the big thing you do in your life to make a mark … it doesn't have to be big to anyone but you."

She nods quickly. "Yeah, of course I know that."

But she wants to impress her dad. I've picked up on that in a lot of conversation threads. He pushed his sister, Ms. Edwards, to get Court a job at a prestigious high school, and he was excited when she got the position at Reagan because it meant a step up on her way to something better. She smiles proudly when she talks about that. Even though it's different from her own personal goals, it's a hard thing for her to let go of.

I slide my hand down into hers, wrapping it around hers in a friendly way and ignoring the temptation to interlock our fingers. "Thanks for coming over, Court."

She smiles up at me, and my heart dances around like a quarterback trying to outrun a defensive end and get off the good pass. I'm gone for her, and there's nowhere else I'd rather be, even if it's deep in the friend zone.

CHAPTER 8
COURT

I have my first two units planned for my class, a basic outline of how I want to cover everything this year that I'll solidify as I go along, and a decent grip on the new standards I need to cover this year, meaning I feel almost ready to start school in two weeks. So Aunt Sophie decides that I need a celebratory dinner. And that said celebratory dinner will kill two birds with one stone, the second bird being welcoming Eli. Aunt Sophie isn't hiding her attempts to matchmake, and I'm pretty sure she doesn't care.

She pulls out all the stops and has the meal catered by a woman she met on her last movie. Aunt Sophie used to cook all the time on her own. Nothing fancy, but normal stuff. Remember husband number two, who was great at scheduling? He thought a menu plan would be amazing for Aunt Sophie. She says it killed her desire to spend time in the kitchen at all. Even after five years without him, she hasn't regained it. But her master plan to marry me off to Eli is motivation enough for her to make some serious magic happen, and that means calling in her favorite food, no matter how expensive. Homemade smash burgers and buns made from scratch with, you guessed it, homemade fries as well. I sneak one as she's setting everything out on the table and almost moan in pleasure. They're crispy and delicious, and I want to hide the whole batch to hoard them for myself. Maggie, the chef, has already packed up her stuff, and I help her load everything into her van. With Aunt Sophie putting out everything on the table, and the artist behind all of this leaving, it will probably make Eli think that Aunt Sophie cooked for him. I don't think she's going to try very hard to correct him about that.

Eli rings the doorbell a few moments after Aunt Sophie gets everything all set out, and she nods at me to go let him in.

"Sorry I'm late," he says, leaning over to kiss me on the cheek. He's greeted me like this or with a hug since the second week after we met. The familiarity always makes me smile and warmth bloom across my chest. It's addicting having Eli around.

I hook my arm through his elbow. "You're going to love this meal. We're officially being spoiled."

He pulls me close against him. It's something I love about Eli—how welcome I feel in his presence, like I could never do anything wrong, like I never need to impress him. His friendship is given to me so freely. "It smells amazing," he says, walking with me to the dining room.

"Hello, Eli!" Aunt Sophie hurries toward him when we come in. She pulls him into a hug, and he has to slide his arm out of mine to return it. "I'm so glad you could come." She hangs on to his arms when she pulls away, beaming up at him.

"Thanks for inviting me, and for letting me rent your guesthouse at such a great price."

"You've helped Court so much as you've both settled in. It's the least I can do. How's Mila?" Now she's taken his arm and leads him to a chair at the table. He pulls one out for her before going across from her to pull one out for me. Aunt Sophie shoots me a pointed look, clearly saying I should start dating him ASAP.

We begin passing around the food, chatting as we dish it out, mostly Aunt Sophie asking about training camp with far more detailed questions than I asked. His expression lights up as he talks with her about plays he's run, especially a couple successful ones with names that make no sense to me.

"What are your chances to be the starter?" Aunt Sophie asks bluntly. It's something I haven't wanted to ask for fear of seeing disappointment in Eli's expression.

He shakes his head. "Tucker is a great quarterback—"

"Just like you," Aunt Sophie says, and I nod my enthusiastic agreement, despite never having seen him play.

"I'll be happy being a solid backup." He shrugs. It's only part of the truth. Eli obviously wants to start again, a chance to redeem himself, but he also fears that the slump from last year will continue. He's convinced himself that he's just working for a spot on the team and a paycheck, instead of for the love of a game he's been smitten with since childhood.

Aunt Sophie scoffs, but the gate alert sound interrupts any lecture she was preparing to give. She scowls and looks over at me. "Were you expecting anyone else tonight?"

I shake my head.

Aunt Sophie pulls out her phone and opens the app to see who's at the gate. She taps a button. "Can I help you?" she asks in her polite but firm voice. Most people don't know where Aunt Sophie lives, so fans don't often show up at her house. Besides, her fans are middle-aged women who don't usually try to stalk her or do creepy stuff.

"Hi. I'm Oliver Hughes, I'm a friend of Court's from Reagan Academy."

I blanch. What's he doing here? We didn't arrange for anything. We've been texting since the ice cream night. Oliver apologized for his short temper—kind of. His tone still felt like I was the one who should have said something about us going directly to the restaurant, but I was probably reading into it since it was just texting. He never said anything about what he assumed about my relationship with Eli. It was that one question, so I'm making a bigger deal out of it than I should. Yeah, maybe Eli wouldn't be jealous, but he's one of those perfect guys. He's a freaking pro football quarterback. Of course he's not going to be jealous of another guy being friendly with his girlfriend. He's secure. And that has a lot less to do with his job and more to do with his chill personality.

"Court?" Aunt Sophie pulls me from my thoughts.

"Um, what?" I'm not sure what she asked.

"Do you know him?" Sure, Oliver knows some specifics about me, but Aunt Sophie is always careful.

"Yeah, yeah. He's another teacher at Reagan. I'll go see what he wants." I stand, and Aunt Sophie nods, tapping the screen to open the gate for him, a slight frown on her face. Oliver is interrupting Aunt Sophie's grand plans for me and Eli tonight.

Oliver's nearly silent electric car is pulling up in front of the door when I step outside. He parks and pushes open the door, his lanky form unfolding from the small vehicle, grinning at me. "Hey," he says warmly, pulling me into a hug and leaning over to kiss me, but I quickly turn my cheek.

"The whole neighborhood could be watching," I whisper at him as I force a smile and step back from him, making sure we look like we're just friendly. He raises his eyebrows. "More than a few of her neighbors have kids at Reagan," I explain. He nods and glances around him. "What are you doing here?" I ask.

"I wanted to surprise you. I thought we could hang out." He moves to come inside, but I hesitate.

"You should have texted you were coming. My aunt has a guest for dinner, and she doesn't know about us. What is she going to think about us hanging out together?"

He scowls. "Your neighbor is just your friend, and you hang out with him." The slight emphasis he puts on "just your friend" says that he's still smarting over my excuse to leave the other night. "Can you hang out with other friends without her suspecting anything?"

"Of course." I sigh. "But like I said, we're in the middle of dinner. You should have let me know you wanted to come over."

He echoes my sigh, sounding exasperated. "Then it wouldn't be a surprise, Court."

I get why he's frustrated with this. If we were in a normal relationship, I'd be excited about the fact that he thought of me and came over because he wanted to be with me. Part of that excitement is still there, buzzing down my spine from where he held me a few moments ago. I long for a time when I'm not always on edge about this. When we can just be us.

"But it would keep us from getting caught and me getting fired." I fold my arms. He was the one who told me about the policy in the first place. But now he seems to be disregarding it. Probably because he's not the one who'll lose his job. He's been at Reagan for ten years, and he's a department head. I'm the newbie. While he'll get a lecture or something, I'm more likely to get fired for an infraction like this. Breaking rules right out of the gate? Before the school year has even started? Bad form, Court.

He holds up his hands. "Next time I'll make sure to coordinate with you about my surprise visits." He's smiling, but his tone has a little bit of the chilliness from when he found out I'd been waiting thirty minutes for him.

I try to shrug it off. He's teasing. "Forbidden romances aren't all they're cracked up to be, are they?"

"Hmmm," he says, leaning closer to me again. I take a step back and glance around the yard meaningfully. He rolls his eyes. "Right. The neighbors. Call me when you're done with dinner so we can do something later."

"Okay, sounds good." I wave as he climbs back into his car, hoping that if anyone did see us talking, they won't insinuate anything about him showing up at my aunt's house or that there's more to our relationship than teacher friends. My insides pinch at the thought of someone tattling on us to the administration. What would happen? Would we get a warning, or would there be disciplinary action right away? I haven't been able to find the policy that Oliver told me about so that I can read up on it, but the handbook is almost two hundred pages long, and I don't have a PDF version to do a keyword search on dating. Besides, my focus the last few weeks has been on getting my lesson plans ready for the start of school, not digging through the staff handbook.

I head back inside and find Aunt Sophie and Eli chatting about the start of the football preseason in a couple weeks. Eli turns to me as soon as I step into the room, his expression changing from animated to concerned in the space of a heartbeat. It's the same worry that draped over his expression the other night when I showed up at the guesthouse with the weirdness of that night heavy in the pit of my stomach. I've waved off Oliver's quick jealousy as part of the overall off-ness of that night, but heat rushes to my cheeks as I realize I danced around the fact that Eli is Aunt Sophie's dinner guest. It's because I didn't want Oliver saying something about it again. But that's an excuse. I should have told him, and then addressed his issue with it head-on. I'll mention it tonight when we get together and see if he reacts or if it was a one-time thing.

"Everything okay?" Eli asks.

It's silly that I want him to give me a hug again like he did the other night and soothe the jumpiness that Oliver's unexpected visit has caused. I nod at Eli and slip back into my seat. "A teacher friend from Reagan. He wanted to let me know about a get-together they're having tonight."

Aunt Sophie's brow furrows. "Does he live nearby? Why didn't he text you?"

Good question, Aunt Sophie. I'm not surprised she's suspicious.

Eli has a look on his face that's almost like disappointment, but he turns it into a smile. "Can't you guess why he didn't just text?" he teases.

My cheeks warm again, but I shake my head and sit back down. I don't want to lie about my relationship. Not to Aunt Sophie or Eli. So I take a big bite of my burger and ignore the insinuations.

When Oliver and I agreed to keep our relationship a secret for now, I didn't think it was going to get this complicated. And the truth is, I don't like it.

CHAPTER 9
ELI

The environment at a preseason game is different than when the regular season starts. The fans are here to have fun, it's warm outside, and everyone on the sidelines is looking forward to a chance to show the coaches why they should be playing. I bounce back and forth on my feet, watching as the first quarter of our game against the Denver Devils gets underway. I'm confident I'll get a lot of snaps in this game, even if Tucker started. I've always expected he would be the starter. He's been their starter for a few years now. I told Court multiple times I just wanted to solidify my place as the backup and feel stable in my position with the Rays. But part of me was disappointed when the coach announced Tucker would be starting this game. It means I've still got more to prove if I want to make my way back to a starting position. It's hard.

But I'll get my chance to shine in this game. Preseason games are when backups get their time on the field to prove themselves, and I'll take most of the snaps once the first quarter is over.

I pump my fist in the air when Hurley, one of the Rays' all-star running backs, runs fifteen yards for another first down, putting us in the red zone and only twenty yards out from a touchdown.

Tucker takes the snap in shotgun, dances a moment, and then takes off around the right side. He's one of the most effective dual-threat quarterbacks in the league, and Coach is likely wanting to spark Tucker by letting him run a bit. I'm jealous. My college coach called me slippery, and I can usually be counted on for an extra yard or two when we need it, but my talents lie in my passes.

Tucker sidesteps a linebacker coming for him, knocking the guy off the route. Something about his stride shifts, and he steps into the end zone favoring his right leg. I cringe.

"Dash!" a voice shouts as Tucker starts walking off the field, each step tighter than the last, pain evident in his face even underneath his helmet.

I catch the football someone tosses me to start a few easy passes to keep my arm warm. I'm going in a lot sooner than anyone planned, so I take a few breaths to center myself in the moment. I don't want the reason the Rays name me their starter to be because Tucker got injured in a game. I want to earn that spot back and prove to the doubters from last year that I'm still a first-class quarterback. Hopefully Tucker just tweaked something and he'll be back out after a few plays.

The kicker makes the extra point, and the defense goes on the field. I continue the easy tosses with a trainer, keeping an eye on the trainers with Tucker right now as well as on the defense. After a couple third-down conversions, the defense forces the Devils to punt, and I'm up.

I grab my helmet and make sure I grin for my teammates patting me on the back to pump me up for my first snap, even if I don't feel it. I've got this. Training went well, and I can put last season behind me and only rise from there.

As I run out onto the field, I catch sight of the trainers loading Tucker onto the medical cart. I shake off the dread that comes with that. It could be a precaution. Even if Tucker doesn't play the rest of this game, it's not a big deal. He's still the starter, and I don't need to let my insecurities overwhelm me if I get pushed into the starting spot when I wasn't expecting it.

I get to my position, glad the first few plays called are running ones. It's a chance to get my nerves calmed and get into a rhythm. It's second down and seven yards to go to the next conversion when a passing play is called in. I scan the field as I try to settle into shotgun, waiting for the receivers to run their routes, checking for what's open. Hurley runs a post, sprinting up the field ten yards and then cutting across. He's got his defender at least four steps behind him. I pull back to pass when I catch a linebacker coming across the other way. He might be able to get between Hurley and the pass if I don't hurry. It doesn't help that it feels like the line is about to break.

I pass it to Hurley, coming up short. He jumps forward to grab it, but everything is off and he can't snag it. It slides just past his left hand, and all he can do is bat it down so his defender doesn't intercept it. I huff out a frustrated sigh.

The tight end, Mark Travis, jogs into the huddle first. "You've got this, Dash," he says, clapping a hand on my shoulder and holding it there. "The line is going to hold." He keeps eye contact with me a moment, then nods at the line as they join us. Each of them nod along with him.

"Alright." I clap my hands and look to the sidelines. The offensive coach is giving me another shot at passing. It's third and seven now. I don't want to punt on my first set of plays this game.

Hurley runs a slant route up the field, as does Jackson, one of the other receivers. Like before, Hurley is already a few steps ahead of his defender. I trust the line, and I trust Hurley. Settling back and scanning the field, I wait for the perfect moment to let the ball loose.

Things seem to slow around me as the moment comes. I pull back and focus on making sure I nail my target. It hits Hurley in stride, and he crosses the first-down line and gets a couple more yards before getting pulled down. I grin.

Travis meets me as we all jog up, patting me hard on the helmet and laughing. "What did I say, man? That was beautiful."

"Thanks." I pull in another deep breath. The line's gonna hold, I repeat to myself. I've got this.

I HEAD over to Mila's new place after the game. She wants to throw me a post-game party even though she didn't even come. I invite Court, who came to the game with her aunt, and she asks if she can invite a few people. I check with Mila, who says it's fine, and I relay the message to Court. I try not to worry that the guy who showed up at Ms. Edwards's house during dinner a couple weeks ago will be part of the teacher posse that Court spends a lot of time with and probably invited to come.

Landon comes out of Mila's apartment when I arrive, and he gives me a rueful smile. "Good game today."

"You watched?" I ask, surprised.

"A little. I was grading papers." He grimaces, his expression apologetic. "Didn't understand much."

I chuckle. "It's cool that you watched. Thanks." It wasn't the best game of my career, but I played solidly. I still have some nerves to work through, but the team showed they have my back, and that goes a long way.

"I have to run. Sorry." He waves and heads into his apartment before I can tell him bye.

When Mila opens the door, she looks frazzled. "What's up?" I ask, stepping inside.

She gestures toward Landon's apartment. "We were going to hang out over there. He's got more space since it's just him, but he came over and cancelled on me. Said something came up that he needed to handle, and he took off. What a flake." She blows out a frustrated breath.

"I'm sure he wouldn't have done that unless he had to," I counter. Landon's no flake, but I wish Mila could see that in Jack. He's nowhere to be seen, of course. Not with work to be done. But Mila's mentioned the number of times Landon has already helped the women out—fixing a leaking pipe in their bathroom, talking down the building manager when he found out there were six people living in an apartment meant for four, and other little things that Mila doesn't seem to put much stock in but show me he's a reliable guy.

"What can I do to help?" I ask Mila.

"We need to move some furniture back to create more open space." She calls to her other roommates, and Gianna and another woman I don't know appear. Together, we get everything pushed back against the walls, and then Mila goes back to fussing over the food. One of her obsessions a couple years ago was baking—actually, I thought it was the one that would stick. Mila has always been at home in the kitchen, baking cookies and breads and cakes. It was one of her favorite things to do when she was hanging out with her friends: bake for them and watch movies or play video games surrounded by her treats. Despite having several new career dreams since then, she hasn't stopped baking, and the sliver of counter space they have in the apartment shows it. There are tiny cookies in a variety of flavors, a cake in the Rays' colors—orange and light blue—and a few different kinds of breads.

"This looks awesome, Mila," I say, coming up behind her in the kitchen and hugging her.

She shrugs. "I haven't had an audition for a few days, so I had time." She frowns, but she doesn't seem as upset as she should be about not getting work.

"You going to be okay on rent?" I ask in an undertone. Another reason I need to be careful about what I spend on my own place. I need to be able to take care of my sister.

"Yep." She sprinkles something pink and shimmery over a batch of cupcakes before turning to me. "Landon paid me to make some cookies for a work meeting of his, and then one of his coworkers hired me to make cakes for their kid's birthday party. And Jack's going to get me a part on the sitcom he's working on, so I'll be totally fine."

It's not surprising that Mila's cookies are garnering her side income. I snag one to remind myself how good they are. It's only been a couple weeks since she moved out, and she's brought by a batch once in that time. I'm just spoiled. "You'll let me know, though, if you need help?"

She rolls her eyes in response.

A few of our old neighbors arrive, and then people I don't recognize, so probably new friends of Mila's. The room is already starting to get crowded when Court shows up with Ms. Edwards and a handful of people I don't know. Quiet gasps filter through the crowd when Ms. Edwards enters.

I hug Court first, leaning in close to whisper, "Thanks for coming and making sure I knew people other than my sister and Gianna. You're a true hero." I hold her longer than a purely platonic hug would be, but I can't help myself.

Court laughs. "Someone has to sacrifice."

I lean in to kiss Ms. Edwards on the cheek. "This was brave," I say in a low voice to her.

She waves her hand. "Who can truly pass up an opportunity to be fawned over?" She winks and moves into the room, heading straight for Mila. Mila has only been over to Court's house with me a couple times, but I've told Ms. Edwards so much about my sister, she says she feels like she knows her well already.

"I'm Violet," a woman says, holding out her hand, "from Reagan Academy. Good game today. How's Tucker Jones?"

"Thank you," I reply, an involuntary smile at someone here actually mentioning the game. "It's his hamstring. No tear, though, and they think it's mild. Hopefully he'll only be out for one week."

She raises an eyebrow. "*You're* hoping just one week out?"

I chuckle. "Tucker's a good guy. I don't want his spot because of an injury."

"Fair enough." She steps aside as Court introduces me to a few of the others who came with her. A couple tell me "good game" as well, but Violet's the only one who sounds like she knows the game.

The last person in their group is a guy named Oliver, the one who stopped by Court's house the other day. He's a lot older than he looked from the peek I got of him from Ms. Edwards's security app. I glance over the teachers who Court brought with her, and they're of varying ages, so I don't know why I'm bugged. Because I suspect this guy has a thing for her? He's probably not *that* much older, actually. I'm just the jealous type when it comes to Court.

"Football player?" he says, his voice kind of chilly and aloof.

I'm already on my guard, and his response doesn't help. I realize I also recognize him from the service event we did at Reagan. He was one of the teachers who made it a point to let the players know he didn't follow football. "Yeah. You were at the service project in June, right, with the team?" It's a passive-aggressive way to point out that we've already met, and he clearly knows who I am.

"Oh yeah." He nods, and it's satisfying that his cheeks are a little red. "The kids loved that."

I bite my tongue from saying that the kids usually do. I've never been one to flaunt my status as a pro football player. Something about this guy is bringing it out in me.

I turn my attention to the rest of the group, who are still kind of hovering around with Court, except for Ms. Edwards, who's deep in conversation with Mila and the other female roommate I don't know. I smile involuntarily at the sweet show of friendship.

"Mila makes amazing food, so please dig in, and thanks for coming," I say.

They nod, and it's like I've given them permission to break out of their group confines. A few do head to the dining table and the food that Mila has spread over it, but others join in conversation with Mila's friends. Court goes to talk to Mila with Ms. Edwards, but Oliver hangs back.

"You moved in next door to Court, right?" Oliver asks, his tone more casual than before. Why he wants to pursue a conversation with me, I can't say. He's made it a point to disdain my profession, and he could have gone to mingle with the rest of his friends.

"Yes. My sister, Mila—" I point her out. "—moved in here with her friends, and I needed somewhere to stay short term."

He nods and lowers his voice. "We might end up seeing a lot of each other, actually."

What does he mean by that? "You planning on holding some staff meetings at the guesthouse?" I ask. I wait a beat and then laugh. I shouldn't enjoy making him uncomfortable the way I do.

"Ha ha. Um, no. No one knows this, but ..." He drops his voice even further. "Court and I are actually dating."

I blink and only barely manage to keep my mouth from dropping open in surprise. Court? And this guy? So her hypothetical a couple weeks ago was about him ... and me.

"It's against policy at our school," he goes on. "So we can't tell anyone. Which pretty much sucks."

"Uh. Yeah. I bet." Why is he telling me? Court hasn't even said anything. Could he be lying because he's intimidated by me? But he has to know I'd say something to Court to confirm it. And despite suspecting that he liked her based on the way he dropped by during our dinner, it still takes me by surprise that Court's dating someone so much older. Which is kind of dumb, I realize. One of my best friends on the Cobras, a lineman who retired last year after I left, is married to a woman almost fifteen years younger than him. It was weird, at first, when they started dating, but they're perfect for each other. I'm bothered only because it's Court.

And because I don't like this guy.

"The heart wants what the heart wants, though, right?" he says.

I mean, yes. When it comes to Court, it's painful how well I know this. But did he really just say it out loud?

"I've only had one of Mila's cookies." I point to the table behind me and edge backward to escape. "I'm going to need a few more tonight for sure. So, um, have fun and eat a bunch of food." I nod awkwardly at him and step away.

Yeah, I'm probably biased, but what does Court see in that guy?

CHAPTER 10
COURT

Oliver has made a point not to get too cozy with me at Mila's party, which I'm glad for since Violet came with us. But she's thoroughly engrossed in a conversation with Mila's roommate Gianna about a production of *Guys and Dolls* that Gianna is hoping to get a part in. Violet was a drama kid in high school and college, and she jumped at the chance to come tonight because once upon a time she thought about pursuing acting. Aunt Sophie is discussing something acting related with Mila and another one of her roommates, and it feels like Eli is avoiding me. He and Oliver did talk for a minute after the rest of our group dispersed among the acting crowd. Did they talk about me and for some reason Eli's uncomfortable about something now? I quickly dismiss that as paranoia. It's not always about me.

But he *is* avoiding me. There's no getting around that. We're best friends, and besides Mila, I'm one of the only people at this party who he really knows. Why would he be avoiding me?

As I'm about to go over to the food table, where Eli has been hovering and making small talk with whoever comes over, the door bursts open and a tall guy with thick dark hair and bright blue eyes comes in. He has to be one of the actor roommates, because he has "leading man" written all over him. "You're looking at the future Phantom Hex!" he announces, throwing one arm out for dramatic flair and then striking a typical superhero pose, one fist in the air, the other on his hip.

Mila squeals from near me and hops up, running to him. "You got it?" she cries as she leaps into his arms. This must be Jack, the guy who Eli is worried about Mila living with.

Jack spins her around, and when he sets her down, he plants a long kiss on her lips. My gaze goes to Eli's, and he meets my eyes with a grimace. This is what he was afraid of—something actually happening between Mila and Jack while they're living together.

Jack and Mila's friends are already swarming around them, congratulating Jack. He pulls his arm from around Mila, accepting the handshakes and hugs from the others while she hovers behind him, beaming. Even I know this is a big deal. The remake of the Phantom Hex movies has been in the news for ages, and everyone assumed the part would go to someone well known already. But Jack has all the looks needed to make him a star. It's no wonder they cast him. This is a huge break for a guy like him.

"Tate Ferris is going to be disappointed," Aunt Sophie murmurs from beside me.

I nod. I'd heard that the heartthrob from my high school years was gunning for the part. "Crazy that someone like Jack got it."

"You know him?" Aunt Sophie asks, surprised.

"Just his name. Eli is worried about his relationship with Mila. I guess he's not super responsible, and he's one of the roommates here. Basic big brother stuff."

"Hmmm." Aunt Sophie tilts her head to study the actors. Jack has brought champagne, and he's opened it to pour for everyone. The bottle won't last long in this crowd, so I don't bother getting up to get a glass. "There's a reason I never dated actors," Aunt Sophie says with a smile. She shrugs.

I pat her on the arm and then get up to go to Eli. He's also kept to the fringes of the celebrators. "You okay?" I ask quietly when I reach him. I put my hand on his elbow, hoping to provide a little bit of comfort for his worry. As usual, warmth slides up my arm. Even though I meant to check on him, the connection eases some of my own worries about why he's avoiding me today.

"He doesn't even care about her now that he's got everyone's attention," Eli mutters, narrowing his eyes at Jack. It's true. Mila has been almost pushed aside, although her attention is still all for Jack.

She stands close to him, but Jack mostly has his back turned on her, toasting with one of the other women near him.

I want to wrap my arms around Eli and hug him the way he's hugged me and chased away my bad moods when I need it. "I wish she could see it," I say in agreement. Validating his worries is the best I can do for him right now.

"She's a big girl." He purses his lips and takes a deep breath before turning to me. "I hope this acting dream of hers fizzles sooner rather than later and she moves on to the next big thing."

"Any chance of you getting traded to Nashville?" I ask with a smirk. "Maybe she has a chance at being a famous singer."

He groans. "I don't even want to think about it. Acting is bad enough."

I laugh, glad that I could distract him a little.

"Court?" Oliver's voice behind me makes me turn, and I don't miss that Eli tenses. I'm more and more curious about what the two of them said to each other earlier, especially as Eli's gaze darts back and forth between us. "We're leaving. Are you ready to go?" Oliver says.

I'd rather stay for Eli's sake. If we leave, most of the people at his post-game party—even though it's basically turned into Jack's celebration party—will be his sister's friends, not his. But the way Oliver won't look at Eli, along with the tightness of his jaw, says he's still suspicious of my friendship with Eli. I'm kind of tired of this nonverbal argument we have going on. Oliver hasn't said anything else, not even when I mentioned that Eli was Aunt Sophie's guest at dinner, but there's an attitude he has about it that's getting under my skin. Why doesn't he trust what I say about my relationship with Eli? It's not fair that he's jumped to conclusions with absolutely no proof. While it's true that Eli is my best friend and the person I'm closest to besides Oliver, there's nothing romantic between us.

An unbidden image of the last time Eli folded me up in his arms comes to mind, and I picture him tilting his head down toward me —a full shiver runs through me, and I quickly banish the thought. That errant thought aside, there's nothing going on between us. I'm dating Oliver. Am I more bugged because as a guy in his late thirties, I expect him to be above this kind of high-school drama?

"I'll ride with my aunt to make it easier on everyone," I finally answer.

And still Oliver bristles. "Okay," he says, his tone short. "See you tomorrow."

"First day back, right?" Eli says to me. "Good luck to all of you." He nods at Oliver and then turns to me. "Let me pack up some cookies for you and Ms. Edwards to take home. Most of these women are on strict diets, and these will go to waste if we leave them here."

He moves away, and I try not to scowl at his back. I need to figure out what's going on as soon as I can. Eli, more than anyone, even Aunt Sophie, has helped me feel at home in L.A., and I can't lose our friendship.

CHAPTER 11
ELI

Court leaves with her aunt not long after Oliver and the rest of her friends from Reagan Academy. I don't blame her after his expression went all cold when she said she was going to leave with her aunt instead of him. I push down my anger that Oliver doesn't trust her around me. Yes, it's true, I've been trying to figure out how to make her see me as more than a friend since I met her, but Oliver doesn't know that. Court only thinks of me as a friend, and him getting upset over nothing is a red flag for me. I hope she realizes it soon, and not just because it means I'd have a chance. I want Court to be happy, most of all.

Once she leaves, I rummage around Mila's kitchen for something I can use to take home a bunch of cookies and some of the bread. There's still a lot left, which doesn't surprise me, considering most of the party attendees are actor friends of Mila's. I think Court and her friends were the only ones who took slices of the homemade French bread. I'm absolutely taking home the half of a loaf that's left. My sister's fabulous baking skills is one of the things I miss about her living with me.

When I can't find any storage containers, I turn to ask Mila, and locate her out on the small balcony of the apartment with Jack. She has her hands on his upper arms, squeezing them, and he's wrapped his arms around her waist. She looks up at him, crying, and I abandon my search for something to take the baked goods home in, striding across the room without even thinking about it. That might be a big brother thing, exacerbated by my many current frustrations.

"Everything okay out here?" I ask when I've pushed open the door. It's creepy how much I sound like my dad, and I'm not even sorry about it.

"Jack has to go to Canada next week!" Mila wails, dropping her face into Jack's chest. He turns and frowns at me, looking pained, although I can't believe he's as upset about it as Mila is. He landed the part of a lifetime, and it's hard for me to consider the possibility that my sister's important to him.

I swallow. "Oh. Well …" I'm not sure what to say next. *Good. It's about time he was out of your life.* I don't think Mila would appreciate that.

"Can we get some time alone, please?" Mila asks in a watery voice. "I need to savor every moment."

Gag. "Yeah. Of course. I'm going to head out, so … thanks for the party."

"You're welcome." Mila waves at me to go, so I turn and escape the balcony.

When I step back inside, I catch sight of one of Mila's roommates, Layla, glaring out the sliding door. This is the first time I've seen her at the party, and I wonder where she's been. When she meets my gaze, she forces a smile and whirls away, joining the conversation of another group nearby. I clench my fists. I don't want to judge Jack without knowing him, but Layla's expression makes me wonder what's going on in this apartment and how many hearts Jack is playing with.

I pull out my phone to text Court about this newest development. I already have it typed. *Is it wrong of me to be glad that Jack has to go on location next week? Out of sight, out of mind,* plus a crossing-fingers emoji. I stop before sending it. If Court went to hang out with Oliver, he might get upset to see a text from me, especially after how he marked his territory by telling me about them dating. I delete it and pull open the door of my silver Ford Explorer. I'll talk to her about it later. Maybe.

I don't want Oliver's revelation to change my friendship with Court, but I think it's inevitable. I'm half in love with her already, and I don't know if I can stop trying to win her over if I continue to hang around her and talk to her as much as I do now.

For my own good, I'm going to have to step back.

CHAPTER 12
COURT

Monday is a long day of meetings and trainings, especially when I don't want to be there. I want to be getting my classroom ready or spending some time hanging out with Eli before the school year starts and things get busy for him with football. He doesn't text me all day, which I try not to read into. He's at practice. They have another preseason game on Sunday, and he has to prepare to be the starting quarterback, since Tucker Jones is going to be out at least a week. Aunt Sophie says he might not play any more preseason games because the Rays want to be careful and make sure he heals up properly before the season starts.

I get home at seven, exhausted. When I park my car in the garage and turn it off, my phone dings with a text that must have come while I was driving.

Eli: I wanted to let you know that Oliver told me yesterday that you guys are dating. Thought maybe if you knew that I knew, you could feel more comfortable spending time together at your aunt's.

He adds a basic smiley-face emoji that I've never seen him use before. In fact, the whole text makes my stomach squirm. It explains why Eli avoided me at the party. If he knows about me and Oliver, he's also connected that when I asked him the hypothetical question about a boyfriend not trusting his girlfriend to have a male friend, I was talking about him. He stayed away because he knows our friendship bothers Oliver.

The squirming turns to a pit in my stomach. I don't want this to ruin my relationship with Eli, and he's exactly the type of guy who would tread carefully for my sake. Besides, Oliver shouldn't have said anything without talking to me first. I wanted to be the one to tell Eli. He's my friend. His text indicates that he believes Aunt Sophie already knew but I didn't tell him. I hate that I might have hurt him that way. And the more people who know about me and Oliver, the easier it is for the secret to get out. Why is Oliver so careless with this information? Especially saying it at a party where Violet could have overheard.

"What's wrong?" Aunt Sophie asks when I walk into the kitchen from the garage. She's pulling out a meal kit from the fridge. She reaches for another one and raises her eyebrows questioningly. I nod to the unspoken question of whether I want one or not.

If Eli knows, I might as well tell Aunt Sophie, because I *definitely* want to be the one to tell her, and Oliver doesn't seem worried about who he tells.

"Oliver and I are dating," I say, setting my backpack down on a bench in the mudroom before coming fully into the kitchen. Considering the millions Aunt Sophie has made, her house is more of a basic, homey middle-class home that happens to be in a pricey neighborhood in L.A. and has some random upgrades because she wants it and can afford it. She bought this house with Russ. She could make a billion more dollars and she would never move out of it.

Aunt Sophie shuts the fridge and eyes me. "Oh."

I smile at her apologetically. "We've been dating for about a month and a half, but we had to keep it a secret because it's against the policy at Reagan. I'm sorry for not telling you."

She shakes her head. "That's fine, Court. You have a life, and I don't need to know everything."

"Oliver told Eli yesterday at the party, and I think Eli's hurt I didn't tell him about it." I drop into one of the upholstered stools at the island, watching Aunt Sophie prep the meals.

She turns to me, her lips pressed together, and she nods. "Hmmm."

There's something more to that, especially the way she's eyeing me. "What?" I ask.

She quickly shakes her head again and holds up a hand. "It's nothing. Only my own speculation, and it wouldn't be fair to spread that without proof."

About Eli? This is maybe the first time I'm annoyed that Aunt Sophie's career makes her abhor gossip. "I'm going to take a shower while that cooks," I say and stand up. I peek out the big window in the kitchen that faces the driveway, but Eli hasn't pulled up in the time since I got home. I can't go over and apologize right away.

I stew over the situation during my shower, worrying about Oliver telling people, but more about how I can make sure this doesn't affect my relationship with Eli any more than it already has. Thinking about losing our friendship because I'm dating Oliver makes me sick to my stomach. I can't lose him.

Even though delicious smells waft up from the kitchen by the time I get out of the shower and get dressed, I have no appetite. I check out my window, craning for a peek of Eli's SUV in front of the guesthouse, but it's not there. It was silly to hope I could resolve it before dinner anyway.

But I am going to fix this. Maybe it's selfish, but I need Eli to make it through my first year of teaching at Reagan and all the pressure at such an elite school. Hopefully, he feels the same about me.

CHAPTER 13
ELI

I've been avoiding Court most of the week, and I feel bad about that. Especially after the text she sent me Wednesday night.

Court: Another stupid day of trainings. I need me some Eli time!

I didn't want to commit to anything, so I apologized for how busy I've been and said, "Soon!"

On the one hand, I've been spending more time with teammates. Hurley and I went out to dinner with a few of the other guys on the offense, and Travis invited me over for a barbecue at his place with the families of a few other guys on the team. I was definitely the single guy out, but it was fun anyway. Travis's wife even offered to set me up with her cousin, if that would help me meet new people. I said maybe. It's silly to keep holding on to my feelings for Court, but I'm not quite ready to let them go yet.

But while improving my relationships with my teammates is a good thing, I miss Court like crazy. I miss the way she can give me a pep talk and make me feel better in a few seconds. I miss the funny things she texts about her teacher meetings and how they make me smile. She did that more frequently earlier in the week, but when I wasn't answering until late in the evening every day, they slowed. I miss the way she leans into me when we're sitting on my couch together and how it somehow makes me completely relax with her.

I miss that I can tell her anything and not feel stupid about it. She wouldn't think it was weird how intimidated I felt at dinner with Hurley and the other guys. She'd comfort me. She'd tell me that worrying about Jack shredding my sister's heart is totally normal brother stuff. I know all of it without her telling me, but it feels better coming from her.

It's no surprise that when I come home from practice on Friday afternoon, Court is sitting on the step outside the guesthouse door, looking at her phone, waiting for me. She pops up when I park my Explorer in front. "Hey," she says, and without any other greeting, she throws her arms around my waist for a hug. "I missed you," she mumbles into my chest. Her arms tighten, and without consciously thinking about what I'm doing, I slide my arms around her. We relax into each other, almost simultaneously. She takes a long breath, and though I resist burying my face in her hair, I can still smell her familiar orange-and-vanilla scent.

I need to let her go, save myself and any progress I made this week in trying to get over her, but I don't. I'm trapped here in a sort of torturous heaven.

She's the one to pull back from me, but only slightly. "Can I come in?" she asks, and there's enough hesitation in her question that I feel bad she even doubts the answer a little bit.

"Of course." I step away from her to open the door, and she follows me inside. I drop my bag by the door to take care of later and move into the kitchen. "You want something to drink? Some of that grapefruit garbage?" I didn't fool her long in pretending to like it. Court and I became friends quickly, clicking so easily I thought it was only a matter of time before the romantic stuff would come. How long have her and Oliver been dating? Maybe that's what held her back all along. It's weird, but it's kind of a relief that that might be the reason, and not that she doesn't feel the same electricity between us.

"I'd love some." She sits at the small square table in the corner of the kitchen by the two windows that look out onto Ms. Edwards's cobbled drive and then the yard on the other side of that. "It's nice of you to keep that stuff on hand." She tilts her head at me, her expression soft.

My chest tightens at that look. I'm a breath away from telling her how I feel, begging her to drop Oliver like a bad pass, and then kiss her the way I've been wanting to for two months.

"That's what best friends do." I hold her gaze for a beat, willing her to understand the lengths I would go for her.

She draws a quick breath and doesn't break my gaze. I wonder—I hope—if somehow she sees it, how gone I am for her. "Are we okay?" she asks softly. "Are we still best friends?"

I deflate quickly, but I make sure it doesn't show. "Of course. Why wouldn't we be? Because you're dating Oliver?" I've been going back and forth all week about telling her that I need some space, but at her words I'm suddenly scared that *she's* stepping back and taking space.

"Because I didn't tell you." She has her hands clasped on top of the table, and as she says this, I catch her clenching them together.

I shake my head. "I understand. Oliver told me why you guys had to keep it a secret." I slip into a seat across from her at the table, setting down the large glass of water I got for myself. I reach for her hands and hold them, reassuring her.

Yeah. It's totally just that.

She frowns, her eyebrows coming together in confusion, but she doesn't let go of my hands. "Then why have you been avoiding me all week if you're not mad?"

Because I'm pretty sure I'm in love with you? I sigh, trying to figure out how to give her part of the truth without burdening her with all of it. "I really have been hanging out with my teammates more. I need to build relationships with these guys so that we all trust each other on the field." She nods, and I go on. "But the truth is, I don't like Oliver, and I don't want to rain on your parade all the time. I want to respect your choice to date him."

Her eyes widen. "You don't like him."

I almost laugh at her surprise at this. "He thinks there's more between us, right?" I point out.

She rolls her eyes and shrugs.

"And you've never given him a reason to think otherwise. I don't like that he doesn't trust you, and …" I curse silently because I want to finish this sentence by confessing my feelings, but I can't bring myself to do it. Telling her will mean that our friendship *will* change. She'll have to keep her distance because she's dating someone else. It's one thing for Oliver to distrust her based on nothing, but for her to continue hanging out with me if she knew the truth? That's different.

"It's just protective, best friend stuff," I finally finish. "No one's good enough for you, Court."

She chuckles and finally eases her hands away, picking up her grapefruit sparkling water and pouring it into the glass of ice I got for her with it. "This side of you definitely isn't new," she teases. She takes a sip of her drink, giving an exaggerated sigh at its supposed goodness. I laugh and shake my head. "Ready for Sunday?" she asks.

"Will you be there?"

She looks at me with an expression of mock offense. "Of course."

"Then I'm definitely ready."

CHAPTER 14
COURT

First day of school and it couldn't have come soon enough.

Last week I struggled with how overwhelming the meetings and trainings felt, how different the vibe was from my old school, and how I felt like I was a new teacher all over again. Being able to see Eli on Friday and talk through everything eased so many of my worries. Where Oliver had told me multiple times over the week that I was worried over nothing and I was going to be great, Eli let me talk it all out without trying to make it better. And somehow it just did.

I know their situations are different. Oliver has taught at the school for ten years and knows I'll be fine. He's trying to reassure me. Eli isn't a teacher, so it's easier for him to sit back and listen. He empathizes with me as the newbie, the one who has something to prove.

My phone buzzes on my desk, and I look over at it to see a call from my dad. I still have about twenty minutes before the bell rings, so I pick it up. "Morning, Dad."

"Hey, sweetheart. What are you up to today?"

I roll my eyes. I've told him multiple times that the first day of school is today, since he keeps trying to schedule lunches and meetings with people he thinks I should meet. "First day of school today. Bell rings soon, so sorry. I can't talk long."

"Oh, that's right." He chuckles. "I ran into Austin Conrad a few days ago. He and his wife will be in L.A. for a couple weeks."

"Oh …" I have no idea who Austin Conrad is or why I should care.

"I want to set up dinner with you and Sophie, if she'd like. What's a good night?"

I bite my lip to keep from growling in frustration. "Who is Austin Conrad?"

"The California State Superintendent of Education." Disbelief that I don't know his name and that I can't be satisfactorily impressed shows in Dad's tone.

"Oh."

"When's a good night?" he presses. "This is a fabulous opportunity to get your name in front of some influential people, Court."

"I'm sorry, there's not a good night anytime soon. This is the first week of school, which is always really busy. But thanks for thinking of me." I look up at the clock in my room, annoyed that the bell hasn't rung yet.

Dad scoffs. "You have your evenings free, I'm sure."

"I'm busy. I'm sorry I can't make this work." Maybe I shouldn't have ignored so many of his texts about people I should be networking with. If I'd been firm with him earlier, he wouldn't be trying to pressure me into this dinner.

"Court. You can't pass up opportunities like this. Move some things around and make this work." His tone is firm, like after I got my bachelor's degree and he wanted me to go straight on to get my master's so I could go into education administration right off. He was offering to pay and everything and wouldn't hear of me saying no until my mom stepped in and forced him to accept that I was an adult. I don't know where she is right now, but I can't keep relying on her to bail me out with him.

"I can, and I'm going to." I make my own voice equally firm. "I'm a teacher, and that's what I want to do right now. That's my focus. I'll see you next weekend for Mom's birthday. Love you, Dad." I hang up before he can argue. The phone rings again, but I put it on silent and send him a text message.

Court: Bell is about to ring, Dad. Can't talk now.

Then I ignore his responding text. I need to focus on preparing for my day, not worrying about my dad's career aspirations for me. I grab the notes I jotted down for greeting my class and introducing myself and my expectations to fill the final ten minutes before the bell rings.

A tap on my door makes me look up, and Oliver grins at me as he walks in.

"How's it going this morning?" he asks as he leans against my desk to face me.

"Pretty good. Still a little nervous." I consider confiding in him about my dad but decide I don't want to get into it right now.

Oliver scoffs. "You're making a mountain out of a molehill, Court."

I know I am, but the comment stings. Before I can say anything, he pulls me up out of my chair and into a hug. I soften. Maybe he doesn't understand how the nerves get to me, but he's trying to help. I hug him back for a moment and prepare to step away. My door is wide open, and anyone could walk past or come in at any moment.

"Kiss for good luck," Oliver murmurs, dropping his lips to mine.

Giving in to the kiss is automatic, but I push him back quickly. "Oliver," I whisper, nodding pointedly toward the open door.

He looks sheepish. "Right. Sorry." He steps away.

I take in a deep breath. "You need to take this seriously. I could get fired. It feels like you're not respecting that." I haven't had a talk with him about telling Eli without talking to me first, and I should have.

He folds his arms over his chest. "I messed up. I'm sorry." His words are clipped with defensiveness.

"What about when you told Eli?"

"You're mad about that?" He narrows his eyes, seeming baffled.

"We decided together not to tell anyone," I point out. "But you decided alone to tell Eli. He's my friend, and he should have heard it from me." Oliver's shoulders tighten when I say "friend," and it's all I can do not to close my eyes and take deep breaths that *that's* what he's focusing on. Oliver and I had so much fun our first few dates, but has the "danger" involved in keeping it a secret eroded all that away? "Is that why you told him?" I ask. "To make sure he knew that we were dating?"

Oliver huffs. "He was obviously suspicious. I figured it was better to say something than for him to ask other people about it and spread more rumors."

I scowl. Eli would never do that. He'd come straight to me if he suspected something.

"Court!" Violet's voice rings through the room, and Oliver and I both jump, Oliver whirling toward the door where she's standing. "Come by my office after school. I want to hear all about your first day, okay?"

Everything in me freezes, but I manage a nod. Is that really why she wants to talk to me? "Of course."

She grins and waves, and then she's gone again.

The bell rings, and Oliver and I turn toward each other. "We'll talk more later," he says, and then he strides out of the room.

I'm left with a pit in my stomach again as I watch him. Everything feels wrong with him right now, and I hope we can talk it out and fix it.

My phone buzzes, and I hurriedly grab it to turn it on Do Not Disturb since kids are already coming into my room. I can't help a smile when I see it's a text from Eli.

Eli: Good luck today. I know it's going to be great. I'll be thinking about you.

I take another deep breath as I read it, and my shoulders relax. This is a much better way to start my first day at Reagan.

Court: You're a rock star. That came at just the right moment. MWAH.

Let's do this thing.

CHAPTER 15
ELI

By Monday afternoon, I'm on a high. Yes, Court is dating Oliver, but our talk on Friday made me feel better about our friendship than ever. Maybe I'm naïve to keep hoping something will happen with her, but I can't help it. There were moments on Friday where it felt like she was on the verge of realization that our relationship could be so much more than it is.

We won our game on Sunday, and I felt more like myself as a quarterback than I have in a long time. Hurley kept sending me videos online of people talking about how great I looked, and though I've been trying hard since last year not to focus too much on what people say about me, it still feels good to have that affirmation. After doing a post-game celebration with Travis's family, along with Hurley and a few of the other single guys, I went over to Ms. Edwards's house to hang out with her and Court. Most of our conversation centered on Jack getting the Phantom Hex part, and Ms. Edwards telling us some of the talk she's heard about why Tate Ferris didn't get it. Apparently, they got hung up on contract negotiations, and the producers finally hired Jack to get production back on schedule. It explains why he left for the location filming so quickly.

I come straight home after practice on Monday since I want to hear all about Court's first day as soon as she gets home. Hopefully, she doesn't hang out with Oliver first. I grab a snack and take it to the kitchen table, facing the windows so I can see when Court pulls up. According to the bell schedule I looked up for Reagan Academy online, the last bell just rang. Court will probably have to stay until around four before heading home, so I've probably got around forty-five minutes before she might show up.

I know. I'm pathetic.

I scroll through Instagram, catching up on the lives of family and friends. After last year, I have my private feed carefully curated so I don't have to see people making comments about my playing. The people I follow now know me personally and have always been positive about my games. I smile as I come across a picture of my parents, dressed in head-to-toe orange and light blue and holding a sign that says "Hundred-Yard Dash," a nickname I got in college after running a once-in-a-lifetime, nearly full-length of the field touchdown. I comment about how great they are and realize how much I miss them. When I was with the Cobras, they moved to Phoenix to be closer, but they grew to love the community they found in Gilbert. I would have never asked them to move again anyway. They're close enough that they'll be able to come down for several games during the regular season. Having my family so close to me is the only reason I got through the worst season of my life last year. It makes sense that Ms. Edwards and Court have become the surrogates for that.

I glance up at the window, even though I know Court's not here yet, and then scroll some more. A suggested post pops up about Jack and his casting as the Phantom Hex, which doesn't surprise me. I've spent so much time talking with people about it and texting Mila this past week that the algorithm is bound to catch up.

I almost scroll by, but then I pause when I realize it's not a promotional picture, but probably a paparazzi snap of Jack with his new co-star. It's a grainy, zoomed-in picture of them at a café in whatever Canadian town he's run off to, sitting close to each other. Jack's arm is around the woman's shoulders, and she's pulled close to him. Like, close enough that their noses are almost touching. Close enough that they're probably seconds away from a kiss.

I suck in a long breath and then almost growl as I let it out. Wow, Jack. He's only been gone a little over a day, and of course he's already moved on from Mila.

I'm not sure what to do. I don't want to be the older brother who pounces on the first bad thing he finds about the boyfriend he doesn't like. But I also don't want my little sister to be some laughingstock among her friends because she's clueless about it. Has she seen it? I feel like I would have heard from her if she had.

The picture of my parents feels like a sign. I haven't talked to Mom about the Jack and Mila situation because I don't want to worry her, but she'll know what to do. I quickly dial her.

"Eli!" she says happily when she answers. "It's so good to hear from you."

"I talked to you a couple weeks ago, Mom," I protest. She makes it sound like it's been years and I'm some kind of long-lost son.

She chuckles. "I know. You're just so busy, and I understand. How are things going?"

"Good. Tucker getting hurt isn't the way I wanted to get my spotlight, but I'm going to make the most of it." I know I'm rushing it, but I dive into the reason I called. "Mom, there's something I wanted to ask you about."

"What's up?" I can hear the soft buzz of the neighborhood around her—cars driving by every once in a while and the shouts of kids—so she's probably in her pool, trying to enjoy the day even though it's likely a million degrees outside in Phoenix. My mom was born for the outdoors, and it's hard to get her to stay inside when it's too hot to go out there.

"Do you know about Mila's new boyfriend?" I'm not sure how much information I'll need to give my mom before I can tell her about the photo and ask her what to do.

She laughs. "Jack? Yes. I feel like I could probably fill out his intake form at the ER at this point."

I snort with laughter. "That's ... awesome, Mom." It doesn't surprise me that Mila has shared a lot more about Jack with Mom than with me, although I'd be willing to bet there are a few details she hasn't shared. Like the fact that they share an apartment. I don't want to burden my mom with that right now if she doesn't already know, so I get right to my predicament. "A picture popped up in my feed of Jack almost kissing the actress he's working with on the new movie he just got cast in. I'm wondering what I should say to Mila, since I've been obnoxious about my disapproval so far."

"Oh dear." The sadness in Mom's voice is potent enough to feel over the phone. While she generally agrees with me about Mila's tendency to be dramatic and go from one passion to the next, Mila comes by the depth of her feelings quite honestly. Mom just knows how to channel it for best use. "I'll take the baton on this one. You're right that it might be best if I bring it up."

I sag with relief. That's what I was hoping. "Thanks, Mom."

"That's my job, sweetie. And you're a good big brother. Mila needs a healthy dose of reality every once in a while, even if she doesn't like it. I'm so proud of you for taking care of her the way that you do."

My cheeks burn with her praise, but it melts into my chest pretty quickly. It reminds me of something my mom told me often when the losses were piling up and my self-esteem was dropping. I could be proud of myself for a lot of things, and some bad games didn't need to diminish that.

"Thanks, Mom," I repeat, and this time my voice is a little thick.

We end the call, and I pull up my notes app, adding in her words to my Kind Words list. I look out the window hopefully, but Court still hasn't pulled up the driveway. She would understand that I'm more relieved than anything that Mila's attachment to Jack will be short-lived. Of course, I don't want my sister's heart broken, but that was bound to happen anyway with Jack. Better now than stringing her along. Maybe while I'm waiting for Court, I'll go ask Ms. Edwards if she minds if Mila spends a few nights here. She's probably going to want to get away from the apartment that will remind her of Jack, if I know my sister. And I'll be ready to comfort her like I do every time. Hopefully this will finally be the thing to turn her off acting for good.

CHAPTER 16
COURT

Violet has a box of gourmet cookies on her desk when I arrive after the last bell has rung.

"Ooooo, can I have one?" I ask as I take a seat across her desk. Until I know different, I'm going to pretend Violet really does just want me to tell her about how today went.

She turns from where she's scrolling through an email on her laptop. "Of course. That's why I got them this morning." She turns back to her laptop, taps a button, and then closes it. She scoots her chair up close to her desk and clasps her hands on top, leaning forward. Her eyes beam with excitement. "Well? How was it?" she asks expectantly.

"It was great. I introduced myself, and we did a quick Jeopardy-like activity in each class to help them get to know me, but the kids seemed to enjoy it, so that bodes well." I pick up a lemon-flavored cookie and settle back in the chair.

Violet claps. "That's a great idea, Court. One of the reasons I knew you'd be awesome—your creativity."

"I wondered if it had all been sucked out of me with all those trainings and meetings last week." I pretend to wipe sweat from my brow, and Violet laughs.

"Oh, come on. The one I was in charge of wasn't so bad, was it?" She leans back in her fancy leather desk chair.

"It was the best. By far."

She chuckles and looks down at her hands, then back up at me with mischief in her eyes. "So. You and Oliver …?"

I suck in a startled breath and my eyes widen, but I quickly wipe away the reaction. "Um, what?"

She gives me a fake cringe; then her expression goes right back to that devilish smile. "I walked by when he kissed you this morning. I can't believe you didn't tell me there was something going on with you guys!"

My heart is pounding and the delicious cookie I just bit into tastes like chalk. I swallow, and then swallow again. Violet doesn't seem mad or worried or anything but excited for her friend, and I don't know what to think. "You're not going to tell anyone, are you? I really don't want to get fired."

Her head snaps back in surprise, and she frowns at me. "Why would you get fired?"

"Because it's against school policy for teachers to date," I say with a lot of *obviously* in my tone.

Violet shakes her head slowly. "I've never heard of that."

I can only blink at her. "What?" I finally ask.

"I've been working here almost eight years, Court. I've never heard of that." She spins back to her laptop, grabbing it and putting it between us before opening it up and tapping the trackpad a few times. When I stand up and lean over to see what she's doing, I see the PDF of the staff handbook.

"Of course *you* have a PDF," I mutter. She's searching "date" like I would've if I'd had access to an electronic copy.

"It's on the website, Court," she says absently, and she taps the arrow key to advance past various search results. "Under staff resources."

"Hmmm." Yeah, I should've thought of that.

She looks up at me. "Court. Quin Winslow and Morgan Delaney are married."

They're both English teachers, and I was in a lot of groups with one or both of them during our trainings the last week. Morgan and I even planned a crossover project for our junior classes. "I, uh, assumed that they came to the school already married."

"No," Violet says. "But anyway, why would it be against policy? We've had more couples than I can count apply together to the school in the last few years. Why did you think it was against policy? Was it at your last school?"

"No." I clear my throat and put the cookie on her desk. I can't eat any more of it. "Oliver told me it was against policy after our first date."

Violet arches an eyebrow. "Hmmm." She has the same look on her face as Aunt Sophie did the other night, when there was more she wanted to say.

I drop back into the chair across the desk. "What?" I ask.

"Can I say something honest?"

"Yes." I'm reeling over finding out that Oliver lied to me, so maybe I should walk away and process this objectively without Violet's opinions. But I don't want to.

"I didn't want Dean Bell to give Oliver the department head position. He has a way of subtly undermining people who disagree with him, especially female staff. Honestly, he might not even realize he does it, and maybe if someone pointed it out, he'd work to fix it." She shrugs. "I told Dean Bell, but he said he didn't see it and didn't want to address it. I didn't push because I'm the youngest administrator we have and one of only three women."

The night Oliver was late to our ice cream date and then put the blame on me comes to mind. I didn't see it that way until this moment. I figured we were both tired and annoyed. "Why did you just act excited about us? About seeing me kiss him?" I ask.

"Because I wanted to see him with you before I judged him in a relationship." She grimaces. "And I was excited for you—that you have a solid connection to the school. Honestly, this summer, I've worried about how insecure you've felt at Reagan. I don't want you to go running back to your old school. I need you here, at Reagan."

I stand up. "I'm going to go. I'll talk to you later?"

She nods. "I'm sorry about this, Court. I hate that he lied to you."

"Me too." I turn to go, and then I lean back to grab the cookie. I might want this later. I might actually want the whole box, but I'll have to buy my own.

I go the long way back to my classroom, avoiding walking by Oliver's. I'm not ready to confront him about this yet. I worried over our relationship for almost two months. I think I might have gray hairs from the number of times I thought someone was going to find out because he wasn't being careful, that I was going to get fired for our relationship. He let me think that when he had to have known it wasn't true. I let the fact that he's older and has more experience convince me that he knew more about it than I did, and I didn't question it. I feel dumb. I feel used. I feel humiliated. I can't face him when my emotions are a mess over this. I might say something I can't take back.

And right now, I can't help wondering if that's a bad thing.

When I step inside the mudroom at Aunt Sophie's house, I hear Eli's voice right away. "She's saying that it's all for publicity and it doesn't mean anything."

Just the sound of his voice makes everything pent up inside of me settle. The emotions aren't gone, but somehow they've gone from boiling to more of a calm simmer. But I shake my head. I can't vent about this to Eli. He's already admitted to not liking Oliver. I imagine that the same protective instincts he has with Mila about Jack will kick in if I tell him that Oliver lied to me about the policy.

"Did he tell her about it beforehand?" Aunt Sophie asks in a skeptical voice when I walk into the kitchen.

"I don't know." Eli's voice is frustrated. "She obviously doesn't want to share a lot with me because she knows I don't like him." He turns, smiling when he sees me, and the frustration eases out of his features and softens his expression. I love that I can do that for him, especially since he's always been there for me. "Hey, Court."

I smile back. "Hey."

As quickly as the frustration dropped away, concern replaces it as he comes toward me. "Everything okay?"

Nothing is okay, and I desperately want to tell him. I want him to hold me and tell me that Oliver is the jerk, that the dumb way I feel for letting him lie to me is on Oliver, not me. That I'm worth more, that I deserve better. That's how I always feel with Eli—cherished. Tears prick in my eyes as everything boils back up.

"Court?" he asks softly.

I shake my head. "Just a long day. Good, but overwhelming, you know? Like all my nerves have drained me." I quickly swipe at the tears and laugh. "I'm fine. Really."

He wraps me up in a hug anyway, lifting me up into him. This is the kind of man I want. The kind who knows my hurts and doesn't try to diminish them. The kind whose presence soothes my soul. The kind who will be here for me even when it's hard.

Oliver is not that kind of man. Dating him was exciting. It felt sophisticated. Maybe I could talk to him. Maybe we could get past why he lied, and I could make him understand how he sometimes makes me feel small.

But I look up at Eli and everything shifts. The warmth inside of me I always feel when we're near each other or when we touch feels more electric. The addiction I have to him feels more like never wanting to be apart from him. Why would I want someone like Oliver when I have someone like Eli? Could he feel that way about me? Could we be more than friends?

My pulse is suddenly racing, the way it did in Violet's office when she confronted me about kissing Oliver, but for a different reason. There's heat building inside of me, and it's flooding my cheeks. How have I not realized that Eli makes me feel more than just precious and protected? I'm acknowledging the heat, the racing pulse, but it all feels somehow familiar.

"Court?" Eli says again. There's still a question there, still a hint of *what's going on,* but also a huskiness that has me shivering in his arms. The room is silent around us, still but full of electricity. Aunt Sophie has left the room without even a word.

"Uhh …" I say in response. I have my arms wrapped around his waist, and I can't help splaying my fingers out, feeling the muscles there. I swallow. I want to kiss him. I want to be devoured by him. I want him to be more than the best friend who'll do anything for me. He tilts his head down, and his lips are so close. I close my eyes, because why would I not give in to this?

Oliver.

I step back, yanking my arms away, and Eli's eyebrows jump in surprise. "I can't do this right now," I say. It feels as though my face is on fire. Actually, I think my entire body is on fire.

I am in love with Eli Dash. It's as plain as the soft blue of his eyes.

I whirl away, running back out the door. I can't get to Oliver fast enough, and not because I need him in any way. I can't fight the compulsion to tell Eli how I feel, and it's not right to do that until my heart is completely free to give to him.

CHAPTER 17
ELI

I sit on my couch, staring at a blank TV, wondering what just happened. Ten minutes ago, I was millimeters away from kissing Court, from confessing that I love her.

I love her.

It was so obvious when she finally looked at me the way I've been wanting her to since the beginning. When her face said she felt everything I did. She wanted everything I did.

And then suddenly she was running away. Back to Oliver.

I stand up and pace across the short space between the couch and my bed, then back. I itch to break loose and run as fast as I can down a football field, to lay everything out there. How can I be so close to *everything* with her and yet farther than I've ever been?

She felt it all. I know she did.

This is worse than any other rejection she could have given me. For her to look at me like the fire that raged inside of me could consume us both, and then walk away? Choose someone else? It's worse than putting me in the friend zone.

I yank open my door, because I can't stay here one more minute waiting for Court Edwards. I'll go to Mila's. Sleep on her couch or something. Get a hotel room nearby. Anything but suffocate myself in this room without Court.

I end up at the Rays' training facility, and even though I did a full day of practice already, I hop on a treadmill to run all this energy off. It takes a long time. Every step for the first mile, my brain repeats her name. *Court. Court. Court. Court.*

The way she looked up at me, fingers gripping my back, plays in a loop in my mind through the second and third mile, and I burn through them quickly with as fast as that image makes me run. By the fourth, I'm exhausted, and I force myself to slow down. Tucker Jones is injured, and it's irresponsible of me to treat my body this way, no matter the reason. I have a commitment to my whole team, and I won't blow that up.

I walk the last mile to cool down and then head for the shower. Once I'm changed into a pair of joggers and a tee that I keep in my locker, I head over to Mila's. She buzzes me right up and the front door is unlocked, so I let myself in.

The sight that meets my eyes surprises me. Mila is sitting out on the balcony—the last place I saw her, coincidentally—with Landon. They're chatting and laughing, and Mila's smile is megawatt. I don't want to interrupt it, and I hesitate in the doorway. I haven't seen my sister look this happy in a long time. Not ever with Jack, and maybe that's the biggest reason I didn't like him.

She turns and sees me, enthusiastically waving me toward them.

"Hey, guys," I say as I step out onto the balcony, which isn't big enough for three people. Landon and Mila are taking up most of the space in two old metal chairs that come standard with every apartment in this building.

"Hey, Eli." Landon holds out a fist to bump. It draws a smile from me. "Great game yesterday."

Was it only yesterday? It feels like so much longer. "Thanks. Man, you don't have to watch."

He waves me off. "I'm enjoying it."

Mila snorts with laughter. "He bought a book called *Football for Dummies* so he could learn about all the rules and stuff."

Landon's face goes bright red, but he still grins over at Mila. Can she see how smitten he is? Does it feel obvious to me because I've been where he is? "Mila's been tutoring me, basically. Talking about it all."

She winks at him. "He's a fast learner."

The red in Landon's face deepens. "Anyway," he says, standing up. "Take my seat. I've got papers to grade anyway."

Mila leans forward. "We're still on for dinner?" she asks.

He nods quickly. "You'd only have bread if I don't grill the steaks."

"Not a bad dinner if it's Mila's bread," I say.

"True." Landon laughs. "You going to be around for dinner?" he asks. "I can grab another steak."

I look at Mila. Her face is expressionless, so I nod. "Sure. If you don't mind."

"No problem." He waves and disappears through the apartment. Steak is expensive, so I make a mental note to buy him dinner sometime. Maybe I'll have them set me up on a double date and then I'll treat everyone. That'd be a win all around. Something to get my mind off Court.

"What was that?" I ask, the second the door closes behind him.

Mila shrugs, but it's her turn for her cheeks to flush pink. "We had a long talk. He's a good guy."

I jump right on this bandwagon. "One of the best, Mila. The guy's watching football just because he met someone who plays."

"And he takes care of Layla and the other women in the apartment," she adds. "Does stuff that we need because the other two are, like, clueless or something."

That, I think, along with some laziness. I keep that to myself.

"He told me some stuff about Jack," she suddenly says. "He's … he's kind of a big jerk."

I almost choke. This is a one-eighty from the texts she was sending me earlier, accusing me of tattling to Mom and saying that Jack has to look like he's dating his co-star, Eliza Grey, to create more buzz for the movie. I laugh. "Yeah, I kind of always thought so. What changed your mind?"

She shoves against my shoulder, which makes me laugh harder. "Jack told me that he and Layla had a thing before, but he acted like it wasn't a big deal. Landon told me that Layla's actually pregnant, and the day that Landon had to take off during the party …"

I nod slowly. I don't have words to respond to the way my opinion is diving even lower than it already was.

"Layla was having an ultrasound, and Jack promised he'd be there with her because she's so scared, of course. But he blew her off because his agent called." She scowls. "Like, yeah, I get that the

Phantom Hex part is huge, but the agent could have told him on the phone. Jack probably didn't even think twice about not meeting her, or even saying anything. Some things are way more important than a job, and it's not like he even would have lost it because he said he couldn't meet for lunch until later." She shakes her head, and her eyes fill with tears, but the thing is, I don't think they're for Jack and her. Mila has such a big heart, and I'm willing to bet it's aching for Layla and how Mila's relationship with him hurt her.

I scoot my chair closer to her, making the metal scrape loudly against the cement floor of the balcony. When I put my arm around her, she leans her head against my shoulder.

"Landon is the kind of guy you want with you when you're scared," she says quietly. "Not Jack. He was probably already sleeping with Eliza Grey," she growls, "before he even got the part."

"Want me to beat him up? I know some guys. Bet Landon would help."

She snorts. "Kind of. But I'm pretty sure you don't have time to go to Canada, so I guess you're off the hook."

"I'll see what Landon's schedule looks like."

She shakes her head and stares out at the sky. It's not a bad view, to be honest. The apartment is high enough up that off in the distance you can see the ocean.

"He is a pretty great guy," I say. I peek down at her, grinning when I note that her cheeks are turning pink again.

"Yeah," is all she says. We sit in silence a while longer. It's been a long time since Mila chilled with me like this. She's always on the move, and maybe it's her newly broken heart, but she could probably use a slow-down, a moment to catch her breath after all the big changes in the last couple months.

"Where are the rest of your roommates?" The place is quiet, which is weird.

"Gianna and Logan got parts as prostitutes in some crime procedural, and Ethan's back in his room, doing some online job he has."

"And Layla?"

"She's going to stay with Landon for a while until she decides what to do about the baby and everything." Her face scrunches again, and I feel bad for bringing her back up.

"What Jack did to her isn't your fault. You know that, right? If it wasn't you, it would've been some other woman."

She nods. "Yeah. I know. I just wish there was something I could do to help Layla. She doesn't deserve to be dropped like this. Jack makes you feel like you're going to be his forever. He's so good at it. No wonder he got Phantom Hex." She laughs darkly.

"We'll think of something," I promise. If I could convince Mila to open a bakery, I could invest in it—it's absolutely a sure bet—and we could use that to help Layla somehow. I put it on my mental list to ask Court what she thinks ... and then I stop that thought.

"What are you doing here?" Mila asks.

"Running away," I mutter.

She sits up, her face scrunching as she studies me. "From Court?" she guesses.

I nod. I want to confide in Mila the way she did with me, or the way I might have told Court what happened if it hadn't been her breaking my heart. But there's very little I can tell without telling Mila that Court and Oliver are secretly dating.

"I thought she was finally feeling the same things I was, but I was wrong." I shrug, but it doesn't feel like *no big deal* the way that shrug implies. "Please tell me you have cookies."

She reaches over to squeeze my arm. "I don't. But I could make you chocolate chip pancakes pretty quickly."

I nod toward the direction of Landon's apartment. "Aren't we having dinner soon?"

She stands up and raises her eyebrows at me. "How does that prevent you from having pancakes now?"

I stand with her. "Fair point."

She stops before she goes into the apartment. "Court's a good person, Eli," she says, parroting the way I talked about Landon before.

I roll my eyes at her.

"Seriously, be patient. Things change."

I shake my head. "I can't keep putting my heart out there. I'm in love with her, and being her friend isn't enough."

Mila puts her hands on her hips and eyes me. "Since when have you put your heart out there? Have you told her how you feel?"

I don't answer. I *can't* tell Court how I feel. She obviously doesn't feel the same way. I can't keep being her friend the way I am now, but telling her would mean never seeing her. She's a good person, like Mila said, and she won't betray Oliver if she knows I want more than friendship. It may be time for me to put some distance between us, but it's not like I can quit Court Edwards cold turkey.

Mila steps back toward me and puts her hands on my arms like she's going to try and shake some sense into me. "Court is not the Arizona Cobras. You can trust her, and I know you're all about being careful so there's someone there to catch me when I crash and burn, but you have to live your life passionately sometimes too." She gazes up at me, conviction bright in her eyes.

"I'm scared I'm not enough," I admit. When six games went by last year and we still hadn't gotten a win, everyone shouted that the problem was me. And when I only scraped by with three wins overall and the Cobras cut me, who else was I supposed to blame? I wasn't enough for my team. I'm not sure I'll be enough for the Rays. Court has already chosen Oliver over me. It's more than a fear. It's a fact.

Mila throws her arms around me in a hug. "You definitely are, but you should be more scared of what you'll lose if you don't try." She puts her arm around my back and herds me into the apartment. "Let's make some pancakes and then take them over to Landon's to go with our dinner."

I sigh and let her lead me. There's no way I can admit that my little sister is right. Court literally ran away from me to Oliver.

But my brain has caught hold of the hope Mila's offering. If Court knew I was a choice, would it make her decision different? And can I risk that it won't?

CHAPTER 18
COURT

When I park my Cherokee in front of Oliver's house, I'm ready to sprint up the sidewalk. I've been in the car for almost forty-five minutes, and I want to get in there, tell Oliver it's over, and rush back to Eli and confess the truth. It feels too big to hold in a moment longer. It's like I've known forever but I'm just now figuring it out. Wondering how I missed the way when Eli puts his hand in mine the heat spreads all the way through me. How when he hugs me, I feel like I'm whole.

I force myself to walk calmly up the short sidewalk to Oliver's small home in Encino. It's probably only just bigger than Aunt Sophie's guesthouse. Oliver's ex-wife is a lawyer, and they lived closer to Brentwood when they were married. Oliver has driven me past the house where his ex-wife still lives, and this is a big step down from the two-bedroom home he's told me about renovating with her.

"Court," Oliver says when he opens the door, reaching out to hug me. "I missed you after school."

I put up my hand and sidestep him, coming into the house.

He presses his lips together as he shuts the door and turns to face me. "Is this about our conversation before school? Listen, people aren't spying on us all the time—"

"This is about our conversation before school today," I say, folding my arms. He's doing it again—making it sound like it's my fault and I'm overreacting. "And about the night you blamed me when I had to wait almost forty-five minutes for you. Or about how any time I admit that I'm nervous or overwhelmed, I'm overreacting."

He scowls. "I've never said that."

I scoff. "That's how you act. But most of all, I'm here because you let me believe for almost two months that I was risking getting fired for dating you and you lied. There's no policy at Reagan that says you can't date me."

The color drains from Oliver's face, along with the defensive furrowing of his eyebrows and the annoyed glint in his eyes. I tilt my head at him and wait for an explanation. He swallows and looks at the ground.

When he still doesn't say anything, I go on. "Violet and I looked it up today after she caught us kissing—" I have to add that in there. Another thing he accused me of overreacting about. "—and I told her we had to keep it a secret because it's against policy."

He doesn't look up, and he still doesn't say anything.

"If it's not against policy, why are we keeping it a secret? Why did I spend all that time stressing about losing a job at a prestigious high school like Reagan? What reason can you possibly have for being so dismissive of my feelings?"

This time the silence gets awkward before Oliver finally says, "I'm still married."

"What?" I cry. So it's not *one* lie. It's at least two really big ones in this charade.

He holds out his hands in a pleading way, like he has some good reason for lying to me like this. He told me he'd been married before on the first night we hung out together, but that he'd just gotten a divorce. It hadn't surprised me or turned me off. Oliver is nine years older than me. Of course he had past relationships.

"We are basically divorced," he says earnestly. "Hannah's been fighting me over the money—of course—so it's not totally final yet. And if she knew that I was seeing someone, she'd use it against me."

I'm floored. A bunch of little things have occurred to me since Violet said it wasn't policy. One of them was that he was dating someone else. This feels so much bigger than that.

"How could you not tell me?" I helped him cheat on his wife. I add another feeling to the mix already roiling in my stomach—disgust. And I don't like how because I stomped in here and placed myself in the middle of his tiny living room, he's between the door and me. I might have whirled around and stalked right out after that revelation.

"I was afraid you wouldn't want to go out with me."

"I for sure wouldn't have," I snap. His excuse sounds so immature that I almost laugh at it coming out of the mouth of a thirty-eight-year-old man. I push past him to open the door and flee. If possible, I feel even stupider than before, even though I know I shouldn't. Believing Oliver's lies isn't on me.

"Court—"

Again, I hold up a hand. "You still have things to learn about making a woman feel safe and loved. I'd suggest working on that before trying to date again." I slam the door shut behind me, and this time I do sprint down the sidewalk. Maybe it's because I was so caught up in keeping Oliver a secret that I didn't see the obvious difference in my relationship with him versus with Eli. How I missed that when I was hurting, I wanted to run to Eli, not Oliver. How Eli makes me happy, and Oliver only ever made me worry.

I pray the traffic won't keep me from getting back to Eli quickly. If he's not ready to love me the way I do him, I'll wait. A guy like him is worth fighting for, and I'm going to let him know it.

CHAPTER 19
ELI

Court calls while I'm sitting out on Landon's larger balcony eating dinner with him and Mila. I tell myself I don't answer because it would be rude to answer the phone in the middle of dinner, even though Mila gives me a look.

I'm not avoiding Court. It's that Mila has me thinking that the next time I talk to Court, I'm going to have to say something, and I'm not quite sure if I'm ready for that.

The missed call is followed up by a text.

Court: Are you home? I need to talk to you ASAP.

I stuff my phone back in my pocket without replying. I can't do this with her. I can't be her safe place while she's running off to be with someone else. She needs to realize she should be turning to Oliver for the comfort she gets from me. Or she needs to realize that there's a reason she's seeking me out instead of her boyfriend.

Once we finish dinner, I send back a reply.

Eli: Sorry, I'm at Mila's for dinner.

Her response is immediate, like she's been waiting for me. I'm intrigued about what's going on. And maybe I'm playing games with her. I feel bad about that, but I want her to understand that I can't be at her beck and call.

Court: When will you be home?

I squint at my phone. Is something wrong with her or Ms. Edwards? My finger hovers over her picture at the top of the message window, ready to call her to make sure everything's okay, but I stop myself. She has Oliver, her boyfriend, to emotionally support her through things like this. If it's urgent, she'll tell me over text.

I slide the phone back into my pocket, ignoring Mila's dirty looks, and put my focus back on participating in the conversation. I don't answer Court until I excuse myself from Landon's an hour later, giving him and Mila some time to talk alone. I'll matchmake those two all day long if it means Mila will finally date someone who stands a chance at being worthy of her.

Eli: Sorry, I'm staying at Mila's tonight. Landon told her some stuff about Jack today that made her believe how much of a jerk he is.

I'll let her infer the reason why I'm staying, even if it's me who needs to be here, not Mila who needs me here.

Court: Oh ... tell her I'm so sorry. But I'm glad she saw the light.
Court: Does this mean she's moving back in with you?

There's no way to interpret how she'd feel about me leaving, since she doesn't punctuate it with any emojis. I hope she'd be sad, but if I told her how I felt and her choice was still Oliver, maybe it would be for the best.

The only thing I can tell her right now is, *I don't know.*

Ethan comes out of his room about a half an hour after I arrive back at Mila's apartment, and we make awkward small talk while he eats a quick dinner before going to a job at a restaurant where he fills in when they're short on staff. Then Gianna and Logan come back from their day on set, and I repeat my awkward small talk with them before Mila finally returns.

"Landon says if you're going to stay here tonight, you should go take the couch at his apartment," she says. "It's bigger and it's a lot less crowded over there." She plops down on the couch next to me and smiles when it sags and pushes her into me. "I think you should go home and talk to Court."

I shake my head. "I haven't decided what to do yet." I think of Court's question about our living arrangements. "Are you going to want to move out of here and we can find something else?"

She frowns, then shrugs. "Probably. I doubt Jack's going to come back and live here. He doesn't deserve it, but I bet he's going to have so many jobs lined up after this. Regardless, I don't know if this acting thing is for me." She shoves me when I can't hold back the smirk. "Stop it. There's nothing wrong with trying out a bunch of jobs until I find the one that's right for me. Just because you've known you wanted to do football since you were, like, two, that doesn't mean that's how it is for everyone."

"Why don't you start a bakery, like I've been telling you for two years?"

She shakes her head. "It's not that easy, Eli."

"It is when your brother has the savings to back it." I nudge her with my shoulder. Tucker will likely be starting once the regular season starts in two weeks, but I've had enough good games that I'm feeling better about my salary. $900,000 a year is more than most people can dream of. What better use for my money then helping my sister?

"No way," Mila says, pursing her lips at me. "I'm not letting you do that."

"Tell me, how many people have asked you to make cookies for them since you made them for Landon's staff meeting?"

She stares down at her hands. "A few, but that doesn't mean anything."

"And more are going to come in." I've shared enough batches of Mila's baking with other people to know she's no fluke. "We'll start small. A food truck or something if you don't want to risk a storefront right off the bat."

Still, she frowns up at me. "And what if I get sick of it in a year or two years?"

I don't see that happening. It's what she's come back to consistently over the last couple years. "What happened to living passionately?" I tease.

Her expression changes in a blink, and she pulls a mischievous grin. "I will if you will," she says.

My stomach drops at what I think she means. "What?"

"Tell Court how you feel, and I'll do it. I'll let you *invest*," she stresses, "in my new bakery."

She's got me, and she knows it. Hence the wicked smile. It grows with every second as she sees me caving. "Fine," I say, reaching a hand toward her. No matter what this might mean for me, how can I not do everything in my power to help my sister? "Deal."

CHAPTER 20
COURT

It's only my second day of teaching at Reagan, and I already feel tortured.

Of course, it's not the kids' fault. It's the fact that I haven't been able to talk to Eli since yesterday after I booked it out of my aunt's house to go talk to Oliver. When I was lying awake last night, worrying over the fact that Eli wasn't coming home, I decided that it looked bad. We almost kissed, and then I went running to Oliver with no word of explanation.

Eli could be practically radio silent because of Mila. I don't want to be the selfish one who demands his time when his sister is probably heartbroken over Jack. But also, could I just have five minutes? Maybe ten minutes? I expect our real kiss to be spectacular. We might not want to stop for a while …

I smack my forehead, and one of the juniors sitting in the back row near my desk looks over. I give her a close-lipped smile and look back down at my desk. They're supposed to be reading and discussing two different articles on the U.S. Revolution, one written in the present and one from a historical newspaper, and then I'll have them present their ideas to the class for the last fifteen minutes. I glance at the timer on my watch. Five more minutes, and then I can be distracted by teaching again.

Time is dragging today.

My phone lights up, and I look at it to see a text from Eli. I hurriedly flick across the screen to open it up, keeping my face chill. The ten juniors in this class do not need to witness me flailing over a text from my crush.

Eli: I'm bringing home takeout tonight. Dinner at my place at 5:30. What's your poison?

It takes monumental effort not to squee out loud. His favorite since moving into Aunt Sophie's guesthouse has been a pizza place nearby, so that's what I tell him. He texts back a thumbs-up, and that's all I hear from him the rest of the period. Which is probably good, since I have to teach.

I get through my sophomore world history class and try to focus on grading through the forty-five minutes after the last bell rings that I have to stay. Oliver passes my room when I have about ten minutes to go, hesitating outside my door, but I turn my gaze to my desk and shake my head. I don't want him trying to convince me of anything. It's not going to change my mind about him, and it will be awkward for both of us. When I look at the door in my peripheral gaze, he's gone.

I hurry home, hoping that by some chance Eli is home early. Tuesday is his day off, and he doesn't have a service event as far as I know. I should probably respect his five-thirty time for dinner, but I don't know if I can if his car is parked at the guesthouse.

It's not. He's probably with Mila or something. I kind of hate her for needing extra care today of all days. Then I hurriedly scrub that thought from my brain and kind of hate myself. It's fine. Everything is fine. I am not a basket case because I have to wait another hour to see Eli.

His car pulls through the gate at 5:25 on the nose, and I'm too keyed up to respect times. Five minutes early is basically the responsible thing to do. By the time Eli is putting in his code on the front door of the guesthouse, balancing a pizza box in one hand, I'm at his side.

"Let me take that," I say, grabbing the box as he jumps, startled.

"Whoa, Court." He puts a hand on his chest and then pushes open the door as the lock disengages.

"Sorry." I shrug at him.

"Excited for pizza?" he teases, holding the door open as I walk through. His heart isn't in the tease, though, and it makes my chest tighten. What if I broke our friendship and any chance I have of convincing him to love me back?

"Of course. And to see you. It feels like forever since last night." I clasp my hands in front of me, trying to refrain from bouncing on my toes. "How's Mila?"

Eli has turned away from me, his shoulders bunched together. He drops his big duffel bag at the foot of his bed. Even though it's his day off, he probably got in a short workout today. As far as I know, the coaches haven't announced who's starting next Sunday, so he's probably trying to get ahead and increase his chances of being the starter. "She's actually a lot better than I expected—"

"Good, good." I don't have time for small talk, and Eli's eyebrows jump at my interruption. "Listen, there's something I really need to tell you. I've been waiting all day."

A resigned look passes over his face, and he sits on the end of his bed. "Oh yeah?"

This is what I was afraid of, that my running out last night and my stupidity in not explaining first has ruined everything. I forge ahead anyway.

"I went to Oliver's house last night to break up with him," I say. Eli stands, blinking at me. "He lied to me, but it doesn't even matter. I don't know how I didn't see it before, but I'm in love with you. Head over heels, actually. Waiting all day to tell you that has been the worst—"

I'm cut off by Eli wrapping me in his arms and pressing his lips to mine. It's everything I hoped it would be based on my heated reaction to him the night before. With his hands on my hips, he backs me up to the wall next to his door, and then he lifts his hands to cup my cheeks. My arms are around his neck, pulling him to me. It's like everything wonderful about our friendship—the way I can tell him anything, the way he hugs away my hurt, the way he'll do anything for me. By the look of resignation on his face before I told him, I think he was ready for me to tell him Oliver and I were engaged, and he was going to let me say it.

"So," I say when we take a breath. "You like me too?"

His face breaks into a grin and he doesn't answer, just kisses me more. When he pulls away again—I don't know how much later—he says, "If Mila asks, I told you that I loved you first."

"No way. I'm not letting you steal my thunder."

"Court, I've been in love with you pretty much from the moment we met. I wanted to ask you out that first day we met, but I thought you were putting me firmly in the friend zone."

"What?" I arch an eyebrow in question.

"You said you wouldn't turn down your only friend, and it seemed like you said 'friend' on purpose." He hasn't moved far from my face, and his gaze keeps darting from my eyes and to my lips and back again. It's ... very distracting.

I shake my head at him. "I was trying not to be too forward or something." I cup his cheeks in my hands and pull his face back to me, kissing him softly, more tender than the heated, intense kissing of before. "I wish you would have. I went out with Oliver for the first time that night." I scowl at him to let him know what I think of my life swerving down that path.

He chuckles, then takes my hand and leads me to his couch. We've sat on this couch together so many times before, sometimes even hand in hand, but not like this. He sits and pulls me next to him, positioning my legs over his lap and putting an arm around my back.

"What happened with Oliver?" he asks. "You said he lied to you?"

It's easier to think about, sitting here comfortably with Eli. It's always been easier with him, and I can't believe I didn't see that. The words and emotions I kept back from Oliver, because I realize that I never trusted him, are a glaring testament to how wrong it was. But knowing that Eli loves me back? It makes it all so much more natural, if that's possible. Something dances around in my stomach at that thought. Everything has changed so completely in just one day. I love him. He loves me.

"He lied to me," I say, "about keeping our relationship a secret because of the policy. There's no policy against it. He was using that as an excuse to keep us a secret from his not quite ex-wife."

The expression on Eli's face is venomous. "He's married?"

I nod. "I knew about that. Well, I knew that he'd been married. He told me he was divorced. It's not final."

Eli takes a long breath in. "I want to make it clear that I don't believe violence solves anything, but I've already got Jack on my list to beat up. I may as well add Oliver."

I lean toward him. "Admit it. Oliver and Jack have both been on your list since the day you met them."

"I plead the fifth." He puts a hand behind my neck, guiding me to him, and kisses me. Once again, I wrap my arms around his neck and lose myself in him. I don't know if I started loving Eli two months ago, two weeks ago, or yesterday. But maybe I should mention to my dad that if I fail at everything in life, it won't matter, because loving Eli is the biggest thing I'll ever do.

EPILOGUE
ELI

I grin at the bright pink box as I use a spatula to slide four raspberry cheesecake cookies inside. We're parked in the parking lot of Reagan Academy. Court has been advising the homecoming committee, and this is their fundraising event. It's also the grand opening of Sweet Kisses Bakery, and Mila's line is five times as long as any of the other food trucks and booths here tonight.

"What's that smirk for?" Mila asks from where we're boxing up the orders at the back of the truck. Layla, sitting on a stool so she's not on her feet too much, takes orders alongside Landon at the window. He's tossed more than a few of his own proud looks at Mila over the course of the half hour she's been open. Layla is a full-fledged employee. Landon and I are volunteers for tonight.

"Told you," I say, handing the box up to Layla, who calls out the number I've scrawled on top of the box.

Mila shakes her head. "Seventy-five percent of the people in this line are here because my superstar football-playing brother told them to come."

I glance at the iPad between me and Mila. "I've got number 42," I say. "Superstar?" I scoff and reach for another box.

"Obviously," says a voice from the open door on the back side of the truck. Court grins at us, and I shake my head. Tucker Jones's hamstring injury is still giving him issues, so I'm getting more time and more starts than I expected. Yeah, it's not the way I wanted to prove myself this season, but the fans like me and so do the coaches. It feels good. But superstar is a stretch. Even if I like it coming from the lips of my girlfriend.

"Take a break," Mila says to me, nodding at Court. "I know she wants to show off her hard work to you too."

"Let me do a few more boxes first," I protest. The line keeps getting longer. The excitement in Mila's step from moment one is proof that this is what she's meant to do. Even if it is just for a year or two. I love seeing her this happy. I love seeing that happiness validated by the number of customers eager for her baked goods.

Mila waves me off. "The other twenty-five percent of the people in this line are here to get a peek of you doing manual labor in a food truck. Things will slow down if you take your business to other booths, which you should be doing anyway. Aren't you one of Court's headliners?"

I roll my eyes. No, not exactly, but I should walk around and sign some autographs. "Fine." I step outside and stand next to Court.

"Thanks, Mila." Court grins at her and puts an arm around my waist to guide me away. "Let her do her thing without her big brother managing things," she says in a low voice.

"I was not managing things. This is all her," I protest.

"But you're hovering. Give her the moment, Eli." Court leans into me.

"I know, I know. But honestly, it's because I can't get enough of how happy she looks. Cross my heart." I slide my hand down into Court's as we start to make the rounds of the other businesses.

"It is pretty awesome," Court agrees, turning back. "And just think, you only had to admit your feelings for your best friend to make it happen." She winks at me. Despite finding out that Court was the one to say she loved me first, Mila still went through with our deal.

I swing Court around in front of me and plant a quick kiss on her lips. "Best decision I ever made, and not just because of the cookies."

She stands on her tiptoes for another peck. "The cookies are really good, though."

"Not better than this," I murmur, forgetting about everyone else around us and holding my girlfriend close. I can't think of anything better than this.

Get a FREE novella!
Sign up for Raneé S. Clark news and get *Finding Taylor*, the prequel to *Roxy's Song*.
SIGN UP HERE!

Thank you so much for reading Eli and Court's story! If you enjoyed the book, please consider leaving a review on Amazon. Reviews are vital to the success of a book, so thank you!
Follow me on social media for news about this new series and more football + Jane Austen books!

LISTEN FOR FREE!

You can listen to Love in Little River audio for FREE on YouTube!

Roxy's Song
Dating Dru
Catching Coy
Hallie's Hero
and
Battling Ben
are now available!

MORE FROM RANEÉ S. CLARK!

Love in Little River
Roxy's Song
Book 1
Dating Dru
Book 2
Catching Coy
Book 3
Hallie's Hero
Book 4
June's Forever
Book 5
Addy's Prince Charming
Book 6
Battling Ben
Book 7

Finding Taylor
Love in Little River Prequel Novella

———

Playing for Keeps Series
Playing for Keeps
Double Play
Love, Jane
Meant for You

Historical Romance
Beneath the Bellemont Sky
The Heiress and the Boy Next Door
A Lady's Promise

ABOUT THE AUTHOR

In a house overrun by boys, it shouldn't come as a surprise that Raneé loves football and enjoys watching (and playing!) other sports as well, like basketball and baseball. When she's not chauffeuring three busy boys to various activities (and sometimes while she is!), Raneé is either writing, reading (usually romance), obsessing over clothes in the form of her online boutique, or figuring out how to get a Crumbl cookie in rural Wyoming. When her real-life love interest can drag her away from imaginary worlds, she doesn't mind spending some time with him in the great outdoors that he loves.

You can find out more about Raneé's writing on Facebook and Instagram.

Made in the USA
Las Vegas, NV
11 October 2024